A 25th CENTURY DOGFIGHT

Wilma Deering's Starfighter went into its automatically programmed maneuvers, rolling across the sky. The marauder craft followed, matching move for move.

Buck watched in shock, flicked on his radio, shouted at Wilma, "Take it down, Colonel! Straight down! Don't roll! Throw on your space-flaps!"

"I can't!" Wilma cried in response. "It's against all the principles of modern space combat!"

And the sky began to explode all around her.

Buck's ship flashed across the sky, streaking to a point above the maneuvering pair. Buck dived, swung through a difficult Immelmann, streaked toward the marauder from nine o'clock, and pressed his firing stud once, twice.

The marauder blossomed into flame. For once Buck was able to grin . . . as was the pilot of the rescued Starfighter, Colonel Wilma Deering!

Buck pulled his Starfighter alongside Wilma's, tossed her an old-fashioned thumbs-up salute, then streaked away, leaving the colonel to reexamine her notions of military doctrine—and her feelings about Captain William "Buck" Rogers!

BUCK ROGERS
IN THE 25TH CENTURY

Addison E. Steele

based on the story and teleplay by
GLEN A. LARSON and LESLIE STEVENS

A DELL BOOK

Published by
Dell Publishing Co., Inc.
1 Dag Hammarskjold Plaza
New York, New York 10017

This work is based on the teleplay by Glen A. Larson
and Leslie Stevens

ISBN: 0-440-10843-8

Printed in the United States of America
First printing—November 1978

BUCK ROGERS
IN THE 25TH CENTURY

PROLOGUE: 1987

The spaceship, standing tall and proud in the early morning sunlight at Cape Canaveral, Florida, was the most advanced production of Free World technology. Its lines were clean. Its command module was functional, efficient, manufactured to the micromillimeter by the most brilliant engineers, the most expensive machinery, and with the most sophisticated techniques that mankind had ever conceived.

Its engines were a dream, designed for maximum power efficiency, control, economy, smoothness of operation, and versatility of performance.

The engineers had said it was impossible to design engines that would meet all those criteria. The comptrollers had said it was far too expensive. The politicians had said, "Our priorities are all wrong!

We need to rebuild the cities, feed starving nations, clean up the air and the oceans, the rivers and the land."

The politicians were then invited to attend secret high-level briefings. Limousines that burned black gold at the rate of five miles to the gallon, black gold that cost almost four dollars a gallon in 1987, carried them through back streets past hushed onlookers on Pennsylvania Avenue, to the White House. A presidential aide greeted them under the front portico and guided them to an executive conference room.

The presidential aide disappeared shortly after the politicians arrived. He returned, now, carrying briefing materials that he distributed to the senators. Each senator received a packet. Each packet had a warning notice rubber-stamped on its cover in glaring incandescent red:

> *These materials are classified maximum security. They may not be taken with you. The information they contain may not be quoted, cited, or referred to by you in public or in private, in any medium or manner, directly or indirectly, under maximum legal penalty.*

The senators were given a few minutes to familiarize themselves with the contents of the briefing packets. No discussion was permitted.

The presidential aide disappeared still again and then returned in advance of the President himself.

The President was neatly dressed, freshly shaved, smiling, optimistic. He was a convincing actor—but senators are good actors, too. They saw through his bright exterior.

The President made an opening statement. The senators responded with questions. What they had learned at State, at the Pentagon, at Intelligence, here at the White House—all pointed in one direction. The President did not need to plead, did not need to exert any of the famous charm—or the infamous pressure-tactics—that had brought him to his elevated position.

The President told the senators the bald truth, and they went back to the Senate and voted money.

NASA and all of NASA's contractors then worked feverishly for months, around the clock.

And now the spaceship stood glittering in the morning sunlight. Inland, rows of palmettos and calamander trees hissed softly in a light zephyr. Out to sea, over the Atlantic, gulls swooped and hovered in the clear, salt-tanged air. There were no fishing boats, no rich men's yachts, no sight-seeing craft in the takeoff lane.

Reaction materials, engine exhausts, staging particles might drop there. Anyone caught beneath a rocket as it thundered into the sky was in dire peril of catching a thousand-ton cylinder of metals and plastics and more exotic materials in his startled little lap.

Inside the spaceship, one man worked alone through the checklist of switches and controls, safety measures, computer programs, instrument readouts, telemetering connections, knobs, dials, indicators. His earphones brought him a constant stream of instructions and questions and comments from Mission Control. Into a tiny microphone he almost whispered the readings and responses that Mission Control expected.

Hundreds of tiny probes picked up his skin temperature, blood pressure, respiration rate, eyeball motion, heart action, muscle tension, nerve conditions, even his brain waves. Inside the Mission Control tower these and scores more were displayed on video tubes that glowed with an eerie light while automatic pens traced out a permanent record of the astronaut's condition on long sheets of paper that rolled slowly past their tips—lines in red, green, blue, black, purple, crossing and recrossing each other as they danced and jiggled across the endlessly unrolling plain of pale turquoise squares.

High over the Atlantic a complex game of hide-and-seek was taking place. American space satellites were linked into the spaceship-Mission Control net, ready to relay telemetered information, take observations, provide data. Simultaneously, foreign hunter-killer satellites sought out the American instrumentation and communication satellites, invisible laser beams flashing when one came into range; a destroyed satellite would not plummet, meteorlike, to Earth. It would remain in orbit, calmly circling the Earth for years or even centuries until its path slowly decayed and it burned up in the thicker air closer to the surface. But meanwhile, it would be dead.

At the same time, foreign spy-satellites tried electronically to tap into the communication between the astronaut in his ship and the hundreds of engineers and flight controllers who sat at their consoles reading *their* instruments and dials, switching *their* toggles and knobs, checking off *their* logbooks . . . and listening to the near-whispered words of the pilot in the spaceship, whispering back answers to his questions, checking and double- and triple-checking every variable in the procedure.

There was one funny thing about it all.

The astronaut—blue-eyed, short-haired, muscled with the lithe strength of a trained gymnast rather than the bulging brute power of a weight-lifter—sometimes hummed a little tune under his breath. It was an old tune. It was the tune of a song written before the astronaut's father was ever born, written when his grandfather was a little boy. It was a funny, infectious tune, and it had words to it that occasionally broke through the humming, to the startlement of NASA flight controllers and, we can be certain, to the absolute bafflement of anybody sitting on another continent, sifting through the static and electronic background noise of a spy satellite orbiting over Cape Canaveral, Florida and eavesdropping on the exchanges between the astronaut and his flight controllers.

He was singing, now and then, a funny little song about a wonderful town, a toddling town, a town where a man even danced with his wife. Chicago, that was the town. Chicago.

The world teetered between poverty and wealth, between famine and plenty, between tyranny and freedom; it teetered between peace and war.

High over the Atlantic an enemy hunter-killer satellite zeroed in on an American telemetry relay satellite. The hunter-killer automatically adjusted its sights and focussed its laser-projector preparatory to disabling the relay satellite. At the same time an American counter-hunter-killer satellite detected the enemy device and switched on its thrusters to bring itself into better range.

At the same moment that the enemy hunter-killer switched on its laser, the American satellite thrust itself against the enemy device and knocked it tumbling from its course.

And at the same time that these actions were taking place, a swarm of small meteorites spun silently and invisibly on their course above the Earth's atmosphere.

No one knows how many meteors are scattered through the solar system, no one has even made a reasonable estimate. We know there are a lot of them, but whether that means thousands, millions, billions, or even more, is anybody's guess. Meteors are not large objects like comets. They don't move in regular orbits, or if they do, those orbits are seldom known to astronomers.

There are too many meteors, and most of them are too small, and too dim, to be seen from Earth. The largest of them is likely as large as a small planetoid; the smallest, the size of a grain of monosodium glutamate.

And at the same time that the enemy and American satellites were engaging in their deadly game of orbital musical chairs high above the Atlantic Ocean, a swarm of meteors swept past—their orbit a mystery but their present position not much more than a thousand miles above the Atlantic, not far downrange from the launching pads of Cape Canaveral.

The automatic program-sequencer at Mission Control was methodically ticking off the final seconds of the countdown for the day's dramatic launch. The chief capsule communicator was whispering the words so they ghosted into the ears of the astronaut who half-sat, half-lay, all alone in the capsule of the most advanced spaceship ever built by human hands.

"Ten."

The astronaut took a final look at his checklist, saw the proper mark in every square on the pasteboard page.

"Nine."

The chief flight controller duplicated the astronaut's actions, nodding to himself in satisfaction.

"Eight."

Aboard the spaceship the astronaut clicked down the cover on his checklist and turned his eyes back

13

to his real-time booster-condition readout dials.

"Seven."

The direct-coupled communications system carried the same readout information to Mission Control.

"Six."

A thousand miles overhead, the communications satellite, unaware of its near brush with death from the enemy hunter-killer machine, picked up the information from the spaceship and sent it speeding at the speed of radio waves—which is to say, at the speed of light—back to Cape Canaveral and simultaneously to NASA-Houston. Thus the system showed its multiple-redundancy, an almost foolproof method of making sure that nothing went wrong.

"Five."

In Cape Canaveral and in Houston, hundreds of pairs of engineers' eyes were glued to green oscilloscope screens, working as if by sheer will power, to make sure that wiggling and wavering lines kept within established limits of tolerance.

"Four."

Within the VIP viewing stand, dozens of generals and admirals and congressmen and senators strained their eyes to catch the first flaring burst of flame as the rocket's engines picked up their ignition.

"Three."

The chief administrator of NASA, a confirmed atheist from the age of nine, breathed a silent prayer for the safety of the pilot and the success of the mission. The administrator didn't know what the outcome would be; if the administrator had known, that prayer might have been worded somewhat differently.

"Two."

Aboard the spaceship, the astronaut turned his head ninety degrees and peered out the window for the last time before lift-off. His lips were moving, forming the sounds of the lyrics of a funny little song that had been written when his grandfather was a little boy.

"Chicago."

"One!"

"Chicago."

"Zero!"

"That toddlin' town!"

An enemy spy-satellite picked up the last phrase and dutifully transmitted it to a ground station on another continent, where a scientific intelligence monitoring officer raised her dark eyebrows and an expression of puzzlement replaced the usual one of intelligent concentration on her regular features.

The great orange and golden and red flower bloomed suddenly, for the moment silently, on the great launching pad at Cape Canaveral. For an instant the spaceship disappeared, not merely to the dazzled eyes of the VIP delegation watching with naked orbs, but even to the eyes of more sensible and responsible workers watching the launch on closed-circuit television monitors.

Inside the cabin, the astronaut pressed into his acceleration couch under the giant hand of monstrous G-forces that endless months of training had only half-prepared him to encounter. His steely blue eyes closed with the strain. His flesh sagged. His hands pressed against the rests designed for them.

His pressure suit prevented his body from being squeezed out and crushed flat beneath the pressure, but the torso of the suit itself spread and stretched.

Even the astronaut's own name, stitched carefully onto a patch of duracloth and attached to his spacesuit, distorted. It would have taken a keen eye to read the name at this strange moment.

The name was Rogers. The pilot's personnel dossier listed him as William Rogers, Captain, United States Air Force, on loan to NASA in connection with a classified special project under direct White House sponsorship and authority.

Captain Rogers's friends had a shorter name for him, a name that he'd carried from childhood. Nobody knew whether it referred to a bronco or a dollar, but everybody called him Buck.

On closed-circuit video monitors in Florida and Texas, the spaceship reappeared, riding on top of the growing ball of orange-gold flame for a few seconds, balancing there on its tail, then lofting away into the sunny Florida morning.

There was a brief exchange between Captain

Rogers and Mission Control. The spaceship was cleared for staging.

The automatic sequencer clicked in; the ship's computers raced through their stored programs, electrons flowing silently and invisibly along silicon-etched microcircuits, through gates and switches, taking instrument readouts, tripping relays, setting indicators. Triplicated computers in Florida and Texas performed the same operations, compared results, found agreement, turned all lights green.

The first stage of the ship dropped away and the second stage engine ignited. For a second time, Captain Rogers felt the giant hand of the space deity crush him against his acceleration couching. For the second time his weight multiplied, his body flattened, then the engine cut off and Buck resumed his task of checking instruments and adjusting controls.

The satellites continued their deadly game: jets puffed, verniers squirted, satellites turned and slid silently through their orbits. Laser beams flashed invisibly, sometimes finding a target, sometimes not.

Higher above the planet, a swarm of meteors, millions or billions of years old, swept silently ahead.

Buck Rogers's ship, its earlier stages exhausted and jettisoned, its command capsule and auxiliary module resembling a sleek silvery dart, left the

Earth's atmosphere and continued on its course.

Buck's mission was no quick expedition to the moon and return. Lunar exploration had been conducted almost two decades before. Scientist-astronauts had brought back their samples, conducted their experiments, drawn their conclusions, buttressed those conclusions with masses of data, and abandoned the dead, silent moon to the solitude which had ruled her for billions of years.

Buck was to be gone from earth for months, exploring the planets and the deep vacuum between them. He would return to Earth carrying the records both of longest duration for a space flight beyond earth, and greatest distance covered by any traveler off the face of the Earth. His exploits would cover not millions but billions of miles. His was the dream of Verne and Wells, of Tsiolkovsky and Goddard and Von Braun and Ley, of Hamilton and Williamson and Gernsback and Campbell and Brackett.

The outside of Buck Rogers's spaceship was suddenly struck by a swarming hail of tiny meteors. Inside the ship they first set up a racket like a fistful of gravel dropping onto a tin-roofed shack. In seconds the sound had increased in intensity until it resembled that of a machine gun firing at top speed, then to that of a battlefield where rifles and machine guns fired constantly, their ceaseless chatter punctuated by the occasional thud of a howitzer, crash of a recoilless rifle, whumpf of a heavy mortar lobbing its deadly freight over fortifications to drop it remorselessly on the enemy from above.

Inside the command capsule, Buck Rogers had little time to contemplate the syncopation of meteors rattling and thudding against the hull of his ship. The steady orbit of the craft was jolted and shaken by the countless tiny and great impacts. The ship threatened to lose headway and tumble end-for-end.

The meteors must have carried some weird electrical charge, for suddenly the inside of the ship began to dance with scintillating lights. The very atmosphere within the ship was transformed into a seething kaleidoscope of brilliantly glowing gasses. Every hue in the spectrum was there, from strange greenish chartreuses to bizarre purplish reds and blues, from dancing, pulsating yellows and golds to heavy, torpid grays, ochres, and blacks.

Trapped in his acceleration couch, Buck could only watch in consternation as the life-support controls of the ship went mad. Ion-counters and radiation fluctuated wildly. Pressure rose and dipped, rose and dipped until he felt he was trapped in the center of a giant vacuum chamber. The temperature rose briefly to a dangerous high, then dropped almost instantaneously to absolute zero.

Buck Rogers, still lying in his acceleration couch, his space suit surprisingly intact, lay suddenly motionless as a statue of polished marble.

If any hand had touched him he would have felt as cold and as stiff as the unliving.

But he was not a statue, nor a corpse.

He was a man in a state of stasis. Not merely frozen, but trapped in a state of timeless preservation, he lay with unseeing eyes, unbeating heart, unmoving hands, unthinking brain.

His ship tumbled on through space. It might collide by accident with some other object in its course, but space is vast and even the largest objects in it fill only the smallest percentage of its volume.

Buck's ship *might* collide with some other object, but all of the laws of statistics said that it wasn't very likely. No, far more likely it would just tumble on, and on, and on.

Its planned journey of five months would stretch to years, then to decades, even to centuries. To Buck, lying within the metal-and-plastic sarcophagous that was his spaceship, the time meant no more than it does to an ordinary corpse lying buried safely in an earthly grave.

But Buck Rogers was not dead.

Buck Rogers's ship tumbled on and on through the limitless reaches of the solar system. What strange sights Buck might have seen had he been observing as the ship passed the asteroid belt and the great-gas-liquid giants with their titanic atmospheres and families of rings and moons, he could not know. For all practical purposes, Buck Rogers was a dead man—but dead men do not rise from their tombs!

Five hundred years!

Five hundred years passed while Buck's ship tumbled aimlessly through space. On Earth his mishap was headline news for a few days. The newspapers bannered the tragedy of the lost hero and his unfortunate ship. The television newscasters ran and reran and re-reran tapes of his lift-off, of the guidance and mission control centers in Cape Canaveral and Houston, interviews with his flight controller, his air force buddies, his family, his old school chums, the milkman who delivered milk to his house and the teacher who had scolded him for flying paper airplanes instead of concentrating on social studies when he was in the sixth grade.

There were even proposals to mount a rescue mission for Buck. But saner heads prevailed. It would take too long to outfit and launch the rescue ship. It would never reach Buck's ship anyway. And if it did it would only find a corpse.

Better to let the space-martyr have a hero's burial in deep space. Better let his tumbling spaceship carry him to that strange outworldly valhalla where the dead astronauts and cosmonauts of all nations joined in their own fraternity of eternal space travel.

In a week the story was off page one and inside the papers; off the prime-time news and onto the features and backgrounders and the talk shows.

A few months later it was no longer Buck Rogers, but Buck Who? And then he was forgotten.

Dynasties rose and fell.

Wars were fought.

The earth teetered—and tipped.

ONE

~~~~~~

An incredibly antiquated spaceship tumbled aimlessly, out of control, through the blackness between the planets. Why it had never found its way out of the solar system, to drift on forever in the space between the stars, was a matter of cosmic laws. In its disastrous tumble, Buck Rogers's ship had failed to reach solar escape velocity. Falling freely, with no propulsion system functioning, it had reached the farthest point of its orbit and then arched back toward its point of origin.

Decades had passed, then centuries, and now the ship was back, its statuelike occupant preserved as if the strange mishaps had transpired yesterday instead of five hundred years ago, back in the lost days of the twentieth century. For this was the twenty-fifth century, and the world was a different place than it had been in the past.

Buck's ship glided on its slow but steady tack through deep space when there was a sudden eruption in the star-punctuated space around it. The white heat of laser bolts exploded into a ball of flame to one side of the ship, sent it rocking anew, tumbling more erratically than ever as it continued on its own lengthy orbit.

Where had the laser come from? Had Buck's ship found its way at last back to earth, and were there still ancient hunter-killer satellites orbiting in space around the earth, ready to blast down any spacecraft perceived as belonging to an enemy?

Suddenly a voice, sinister and bass in tone, spoke. "That was a warning blast. Retard your speed and bring your ship about or the next will destroy you!"

But the derelict ship continued to tumble on, its systems dead, its pilot unconscious, in a state of complete mental and physical stasis for the past five hundred years.

The voice that had spoken belonged to a dark, tight-lipped man with cold eyes and an unsavory cast to his face. This was the man Kane—known behind his back as Killer Kane. Whether the title bore any relationship to the original killer, Cain, is moot. But in this man's case, the title was apt.

He sat at the controls of a space attack vessel, his big hands guiding the controls with a competence that bordered on contempt. To either flank of his ship a sister craft soared, and Kane, like a veteran halfback directing two powerful but inexperienced downfield blockers as they cleared a path for him, barked his directions to the ships to his left and his right.

"Another round," Kane gritted.

The laser flared. Buck's ship jounced at the nearness of the explosion.

"Closer," Kane muttered. Not only were his two subordinates fighting at his direction, but his own ship was armed as well and he fired his own lasers, pressing the firing stud on his control rod as Buck's tumbling antique came within his sights. The five hundred year old ship rocked and tumbled, unable either to fight back or to flee.

In his space-fighter, Kane commanded his two subordinates. "Stand by to finish him off. Five . . . four . . . three . . ."

He pressed the throttle of his fighter forward. The ship, already coursing through space at incredible speed, lurched ahead still faster, faster, closing in for the kill, ready to blast its helpless prey into a blossoming spray of white-hot space debris!

Meanwhile, the interior of the derelict craft presented as eerie an aspect as ever human eye had perceived. Think of any explorer opening a crypt sealed and forgotten for hundreds and thousands of years, breaking the seals of time, peering within, breath stilled, heart leaping, hands icy, blood pounding. And then . . .

Through the window of Buck Rogers's derelict

spaceship could be seen a sight that might have been found in a deep-freeze. The window itself was frosted, not with condensation on its outside, for space is a vacuum and contains no water vapor. But from within, from the gases that had flooded the cabin in the last frantic seconds of the meteor storm, from the water vapor dissolved in the very atmosphere of the ship.

And inside that strange deep-freeze, the slumped form of a bearded man, his chin pressed against the collar of his flight suit, his head leaning toward the frosted window. And not merely the inner surface of the window, but the entire interior of the spaceship's cabin was covered with a soft, frosted glaze. And in that glaze lay the man himself, covered entirely with white condensation.

Apparently the state of stasis was less than one hundred percent effective. For Buck Rogers had entered his ship a clean-shaven man, and he was now heavily bearded, his hair grown long and shaggy in the five hundred years he had lain in the tumbling derelict.

Kane piloted his fighter craft alongside Buck's ship with competence borne of a hundred space battles, a thousand maneuvers.

Through the double thickness of the window of his own ship and Buck Rogers's, he peered with those cold dark eyes of his.

"He appears dead," Kane rasped.

"Then let's disintegrate him," a second voice

spoke coldly. "Before Princess Ardala's ship sails through here and hits the old derelict."

Kane shook his head. "No," he considered coldly. "There's something about that ship. I've never seen anything like it. No, this may be a prize worth exploiting."

He rubbed his chin thoughtfully. "Prepare to take the derelict in tow. Open a communication channel to Princess Ardala. Inform her that we're boarding a hostile spacecraft, and will report to her later with details of what we find."

Kane clicked off his communicator and continued to peer through the double thickness of window that separated him from Buck Rogers, peering into the sleeping face of the ancient spaceman, peering as if measuring the man and assessing the contents of the ship in which he lay.

Consider this: if some World War II aviator, Jimmy Doolittle or Richard Bong or any of the others, had risen from some airbase in Europe or America or in the Pacific theater, and had come face to face with a Saturn V spaceship just lifting off its pad and heading at five thousand miles per hour for orbit, he'd surely have returned to base, headed straight for the nearest field hospital, and turned himself in for treatment for a case of acute combat fatigue.

They just wouldn't have believed it!

Now consider this: William Rogers, Captain

USAF, lifts off from Cape Canaveral, Florida, on a bright morning in the year 1987. He is caught in a meteor storm above the Earth's atmosphere. He knows nothing for the next five hundred years, and then . . .

A massive ship moved through space. It was not ten or twenty or fifty years more advanced than Buck's craft had been. And it was not merely as much larger as the Consolidated B-36 was than the Wrights' first plane. No, the difference in technology and in size was five *centuries!*

Buck Rogers's craft lay on the floor of a giant launching bay as a wooden viking craft would have lain on the deck of the QE2. And around it swarmed a throng of scurrying figures, a mix of curious technicians and watchful-eyed soldiers. Again, it was as if some experimental Breguet helicopter of early-1930s vintage had mysteriously appeared over the Gulf of Tonkin and landed safely on the deck of an American aircraft carrier in 1970.

The twin reactions would have been an arousal of startled curiosity and a wild, almost paranoid panic of the security forces!

Now, on the great starship in whose bay Buck Rogers's half-millenium-old craft lay motionless, a swarm of inquiring technicians peered and prodded at the ancient spacecraft, frantic with curiosity to resolve its mysteries—while at the same time stern-visaged starship troopers, Draconian

Guards of the Realm, circulated among them, weapons at the ready.

And at the command position stood one whose air of authority would brook no opposition.

Kane.

He looked through the window of the ancient spaceship and some instinct prompted him, as he gazed on Buck Rogers's motionless form, to mutter, "He's alive!"

They moved the rigid form of the space pilot, laid him on a surgical table ringed with bright spotlights. They attached electronic probes, chemical tubes, stimulators and resuscitators to the unresisting form. Powerful beams of a nearby blood-red intensity pulsed in the tubes.

And Buck Rogers's eyelids fluttered!

The stateroom was magnificent. It had the outfittings of the captain's quarters on the most luxurious of ancient sea-yachts, yet it could serve as its mistress's audience chamber, her sitting room, or her boudoir at her choice.

There was a canopied bed, covered with thick, soft, white furs of the most exotic animals, striped and tanned and fitted to suit the whim of their powerful owner. There were pillows and mirrors and perfume dispensers, satin quilts and snow-white fur robes to please the most demanding of sybarites.

Lounging in the midst of this barbaric splendour

was the one creature to whom its beauty, its luxury, its promise of hedonistic indulgence and its hint of barbaric sadism, were all fitted with perfect appropriateness: a woman stunningly gowned, her raiment perfectly designed to set off her long, flowing hair, her rich, smooth olive skin, her dark, slightly slanted eyes, her voluptuous body whose generous curves were accentuated rather than concealed by the flowing lines of her gown.

This was the Princess Ardala.

At a signal from the companionway outside her stateroom the Princess called a single imperious word: "Enter."

The dark figure of Kane appeared, an expression of deeply troubled concern on his face.

His meditation was interrupted by the Princess Ardala's annoyed comment. "What of our intruder, Kane, that is so important it could not await my rising?"

Kane stepped forward with thoughtfully measured strides. "The man lives," he announced. "And why, is a puzzle."

"You don't know why he lives?" Ardala echoed. "Have you brought me this riddle to deal with, as a dimensional puzzle is tossed to a troublesome child, to keep her busy at play while the adults tend to more serious matters?"

Kane shook his head, ignoring the jibe. "The puzzle is for me to decipher, my princess. The ship is antiquated, it's unlike anything I've ever seen in the whole span of stars—for that matter I've never seen its like outside the pages of some illustrated history book."

Impatiently, Ardala snapped, "Kane, get on with—"

"He was frozen, my princess!"

"Frozen?"

"A combination of gases," the man explained. "Oxygen, freon, cryogen." He paced as if reciting a chemistry lesson. "Ozone." He nodded his head, ticked off the substances on his fingers. "Methalon. Almost a perfect balance."

Ardala shrugged her smooth shoulders petulantly. "There are techniques used in cases of surgery and in the suspension of terminal illnesses throughout the civilized galaxy.'

"Yes," Kane agreed. "Yes, there are—today! But this man is another matter. His ship, my princess!"

"Kane, I have no patience for lectures, any more than I have for solving riddles. Come to the point or leave my presence!"

"It's the instrumentation on the ship! It too was stopped. Our scientists have taken readouts from its circuitry, and they indicate that this man and his ship have been frozen solid since the year 1987!"

Now curiosity conquered annoyance in the Princess Ardala. "You're telling me, Kane, that—"

"Precisely, I am! That man must be over five hundred years old, my princess!"

Her eyebrows flew upward in surprise. "You're serious!"

"Completely! The pilot of that ship was frozen by whatever disaster overcame his ship, and then preserved by that combination of gases, so instantaneously and so perfectly that now he is fully preserved and . . . living!"

The princess moved subtly on her fur-quilted bed. It was almost as if a fascinating man had entered the room, and she was arranging herself to display her charms in their most subtle but most alluring pose. "Preserved," she purred. "But—preserved young or preserved old?"

"Very young," Kane responded.

"No—shall I say, *defects*—from the ordeal?"

"Fortunately for the man," Kane said, "we are quite advanced in the science of cryogenics."

"I've never met a man five hundred years old," Ardala almost crooned. She seemed lost in contemplation for the barest fraction of a moment. Then she said, "Prepare him for an audience."

Kane did not assent immediately. "I would suggest that you allow us a little time. We have been inducing massive amounts of oxygen into his system, to resuscitate him. I'm afraid he might babble incoherently for a little while. You know, there's such a thing as oxygen intoxication."

Ardala's eyes flashed. She was not accustomed to having her wishes denied, however subservient the manner of the other. "I will make allowances," she declared imperiously.

* * *

For the first time in five hundred years, Buck Rogers opened his eyes and tried to focus them on the ring of faces surrounding him. They peered down, eyes shining with curiosity.

"Where am I?" Buck said.

One of the faces—that of the dark, dominating person who had just left the chamber of the Princess Ardala—swam into clearer focus. "We will ask the questions," Kane lipped thinly. "Now, spaceman, who are you?"

"Rogers, William," Buck stammered automatically. "Captain, United States Air Force. And—who are *you?*"

Kane exchanged significant looks with the other faces surrounding Buck.

Another voice cut through the conversation—a smooth, sensual woman's voice coming from the entryway of the medical examining room. "What did that man say?"

The faces turned away from Rogers, and toward the newcomer. It was the Princess Ardala, but no longer was she gowned in the lounging robes of her sumptuous boudoir. She had exchanged them for the resplendent finery of the Imperial Princess and Heir Apparent of the Draconian Interstellar Empire.

Even in his weakened and semi-incoherent condition, Buck Rogers managed to halfway raise his head and see who had spoken in the lovely and sensual, yet imperious tones.

Kane said to Ardala, "Something about a United States. Never heard of it." He turned commandingly upon Buck. "Captain, what is your destination?"

Reaction to his first movement in half a millenium overcame Buck. He clutched at his head, collapsed back onto the table. "Oh, my God!" he gasped.

The princess looked on in alarm. "What is it?"

"My head." He clutched at his temples. "Anyone got an aspirin?"

Puzzled, the princess asked, "What does that mean?"

"Probably some sort of anti-pain drug," Kane supplied.

"Give him something to ease his discomfort," Ardala commanded.

Taking his clue from the princess, Kane nodded toward an orderly. The latter moved off to bring a medication.

Buck had recovered sufficiently to speak again. "What is this place? Where am I? Who are you?"

"You're aboard the king's flagship *Draconia*," Ardala supplied. "Under the command of the Royal Princess Ardala."

"Oh," Buck said. Then it sank in. "Who?"

"Never mind," Kane interrupted the exchange. "We want to know all about you. Where you are from."

"Wait," Buck pleaded. "Slow down. What was that about a ship?"

"One of His Majesty's Star Fortresses," Ardala said. "On its way to Earth on a mission of peace."

"On its way *to* Earth?" Buck was startled. "You mean, you guys aren't from . . . I mean, we aren't on . . ." He tried again to rise, failed. "Oh, I'm definitely going to need that aspirin."

At this moment the orderly returned, a hypodermic syringe held carefully in one hand.

"Give it to him," Ardala commanded.

"Hey," Buck exclaimed. "What's in that? Ooooh."

Kane spoke menacingly. "Captain, bearing in mind that you are a captive of a dynasty that has conquered three fourths of the universe . . . you will answer very carefully, if you value your life."

Buck stared at Kane, dumbstruck. The drug that had been administered was beginning to take effect: his eyes were growing vague. "What . . ."

"You claim to have been blown off course," Kane said accusingly.

"Hmmm?"

"How do you explain that you were conveniently drifting in an unconscious state that would take you directly onto the princess's announced flight path to Earth?"

Buck turned his gaze away from the menacing Kane, toward the beautifully and splendidly garbed princess. "That you?" he asked with childlike wonder. "Are you a real live princess?"

"I think you've given our captain a little too much medication," Ardala commented.

"No," Buck countered almost drunkenly. "I feel great." And he began to giggle, and giggle, and giggle, while the technicians stared at him as if he had gone mad!

Later, three figures walked together down one of the corridors of the ship. One of them was Kane. Another was the Princess Ardala. The third was a strange being, a mutant, neither human nor animal, neither man nor beast, but something in between. As intelligent as a human—or nearly so— and as powerful and cunning as the jungle predators from whom his ancestors had been bred. He was Tigerman.

Ardala and Kane were conversing seriously while Tigerman padded silently, watchfully, menacingly beside them.

"The United States of America," Ardala said thoughtfully. "I recall that it was an empire on the planet Earth, some centuries ago."

"Those royal tutors gave you your money's worth," Kane commented wryly.

"*You* are from Earth," Ardala snapped. "Surely you remember its history better than I!"

"The United States," Kane took up the thread. "It perished almost five hundred years ago. It doesn't exist any longer. The man Rogers is lying."

"It would explain his clothing," Ardala said. "As well as his spacecraft and the settings of its instruments."

"I've a better explanation," Kane countered.

"He's a very clever plant from those schemers on the Federal Directorate on Earth."

Ardala stopped in mid-stride and swung upon Kane. "A *plant?*"

"A spy, yes! Placed in our path deliberately by their military, so we would *discover* him, by *accident.*" The irony was heavy in his voice.

"They wouldn't dare," Ardala said scornfully. "We come as a royal envoy to earth from my father's kingdom."

"I am aware of your father's *stated* purpose," Kane replied. "To guarantee trade between Earth and the Draconian dynasty."

"Then why would they possibly place a spy on board our ship?" Ardala asked.

"*To search our ship,*" Kane answered. "To see if we are armed!"

"I see." Ardala's imperious posture seemed to sink a little. She gazed down the corridor and said again, "I see."

"We cannot allow that, can we?" Kane prompted.

"No . . ."

"Then I am to assume that I may—let us say, *dispose*—of Captain Rogers, as I see fit?"

Ardala turned away without making a direct reply. "How you deal with security," she said, "is your own prerogative, Kane."

TWO

~~~~~~

Inside the great bay, Buck Rogers's ship was all but lost in the immensity of the cavernous interior and the massive, complex array of machinery. Workmen were bustling over and around the ship, studying, investigating, restoring it to working order. From one of the corridor portals, Kane entered the bay. He was carrying a small oblong box. He handed it to one of the technicians working on the ship and instructed the worker. "These are computer boards to be reinstalled on Captain Rogers's ship, now that we've studied and tested them thoroughly. As soon as they're reconnected, stand by to launch!"

Buck himself, still recovering from his long ordeal, was wheeled into the bay, rather than walking there under his own power. "Now this is realistic," he was saying, still half-bemused by the Draconian drug that had been injected into him. "What a layout this place is. It looks like Howard Hughes's bathroom!"

Kane stepped away from the ship, stood over Buck's rolling transport. "And how are we this morning?" Kane asked unctuously.

"Fantastic," Buck grinned. "I wish you were all really here, but I know I'm gonna wake up, and when I do—*poof*!"

Buck continued talking to Kane as he rolled toward his ship. "Say, what a coincidence! I have a ship just like that one."

Kane shot a significant glance to one of Buck's medical orderlies. "You can discontinue medication now," Kane commanded.

"No," Buck countered. "Leave it on. I love it."

"You'll be on your way shortly," Kane muttered.

Buck said, "Great! Where are we going?"

"You're going home," Kane answered.

"Great. Where's that?"

"Earth."

"Oh. Right."

They had arrived at the ship. The orderlies helped Buck to a sitting posture. He heard Kane continuing to speak. "Your ship has been serviced and its computers reprogrammed to take you home. I'm sure you must be very anxious to get back."

"Oh, yeah," Buck said. "I feel like I must have been gone for weeks. Weeks and weeks and weeks." He started to climb down from the rolling cart but his knees buckled beneath him. Orderlies sprang forward to keep him from falling.

"Whoo-eee!" Buck grabbed his head. "I must've had some good time with you guys. Gonna miss you. Say, why don't we all go on down there to-gether?"

"No, Captain," Kane said, "you go on ahead. But don't worry, we'll follow in just a few days."

"Not if I wake up," Buck grinned. "Poof!"

An orderly at either side, Buck was helped through the boarding hatch into his ancient space-ship. "Guess I'll be seeing you. I mean you're going to be hard to miss coming down in this thing. Piece of advice," he grinned. "Don't try landing at New York. They weren't even too crazy about the Concorde." Again, Buck burst into giggles. The others remained serious.

"Say," Buck complained, "I guess you guys can't fix everything. My chronometer's still acting whacky. Seems to say that I've been gone for five hundred years. Hahaha!" As Buck's laughter echoed through the great bay, Kane nodded to a crew of technicians. They slammed shut the board-ing hatch on Buck's spaceship and locked it with all seals down.

Inside the ship, Buck muttered to himself. "Boy, are they going to be surprised back at Houston when I show up with this story. Talk about deep-space rapture making you hallucinate!"

And the ancient spaceship blasted through the opened doors of the giant bay, back to the blackness and emptiness from which it had been retrieved after its journey of half a millenium.

As Buck's ship shrank from a spacecraft to a tiny point of gleaming light, the Princess Ardala peered after it, her thoughts lost in the distant stars. Her giant Tigerman bodyguard loomed powerfully behind her, and Kane advanced to parley with his princess.

"Is it possible?" Ardala asked. "Could he really have come through space from the Earth of five hundred years ago?"

"Yes," Kane nodded. "It's just possible. Precisely why I believe it to be an ingenious plan to dupe us, undoubtedly masterminded by Doctor Huer. Well, we will turn this little charade against its creator!"

"Against him? Why? How?" Ardala asked.

"He has given us the perfect opportunity to test the Earth's defense shield."

"What do you mean, test it? We know that anything approaching Earth without clearance is immediately incinerated."

"But if our captain is a spy," Kane purred, "as I suspect he is . . . they will escort him through the shield. Along the narrow channel known only to their military."

"But," Ardala demanded, "how will that help us?"

"I've hidden a microtransmitter aboard Captain Rogers's ship," Kane explained. "There's no way he can detect its presence—I had our techs build it into his computer's circuits. When they take him down, the transmitter will be giving us the equivalent of a guide map. When we give the signal, that map will be used by your father's forces to pour through their defensive shield."

Ardala looked up into Kane's face, admiration filling her own. "You are clever, Kane!"

"A perfect combination," he responded. "Your throne and my ability. We will one day rule your father's kingdom!"

"Don't be so eager to unseat my father," Ardala snapped. "What if our captain is *not* a spy—what happens then?"

Kane shrugged. "Then he burns."

Ardala looked away oddly. "I see."

"You don't look pleased," Kane said.

"Of course I'm pleased. It's just that . . . I had the strangest feeling that . . . I'd meet Captain Rogers again, somewhere." Ardala looked away from Kane, a wistful expression on her beautiful features.

Inside his spaceship, Buck Rogers was functioning as a space pilot for the first time in half a thousand years. His skillful fingers switched controls, flipped levers as he ran through his pre-touchdown checklist. He was thoroughly enjoying his last hours in space, singing half-aloud as he worked.

"I'm flying down . . . I'm getting down . . . down, down, down . . . to my kind of town!" He broke off his song and switched on his transmitter. "Houston Control," he snapped in businesslike terms. "This is astro-flight 711. Put down the cards and the

42

backgammon boards and get on the horn to me. Buck is back—Lucky Buck!"

Buck switched off his transmitter, turned up the receiver of his radio set. It whined and blasted out amplified static, but there was no voice in reply to his own. "Hello," Buck tried again. "Houston control! Hello! What say, guys? Do you read . . . ?"

On the Earth below the results of half a thousand years of history lay spread across the face of the planet, across her continents and her oceans; no square foot of Earth's face was untouched by the hands of humankind, from polar ice cap to equatorial desert, from ice-capped mountain peak to steaming, green jungle.

In some places the hand of man had wrought beauty.

In others—horror.

Inside a towering city of the twenty-fifth century, inside one of the great supermodern buildings, there was a room . . . a strange room with no discernible walls. Only planes of velvety blackness, strange, deep velvety blackness, and on the blackness, outlines and points of light, lights that represented the stars surrounding Earth. And on the floor of the strange room, a gridwork of coordinates with pinpoints of gleaming color moving back and forth, left and right.

This strange room was unknown to most of the inhabitants of earth. Ninety-nine percent of humanity had never heard of this strange place, and the one percent who knew of its existence spoke of it in hushed whispers, glancing furtively about to make certain that their statements were not over-heard.

This was the War Room.

Inside the War Room a technican's eyes wid-ened as she saw the light moving across the face of her 'scope. She was unconscious of the curves of her body, of how they were emphasized by her trim, form-fitting tunic and tight-cut military trousers. She thought only of her duty, of the re-sponsibilities which she bore.

"Uh, sir . . ." the technician said aloud. "Su-per. . . ."

Her supervisor, a similarly uniformed technician wearing the unisex garb of his assignment, turned at the sound of her voice. "Super here," he spoke into a mouthpiece. "What station is this?"

"Delta Vector, Supervisor." A momentary pause. "You don't hear from me very often. My scanners monitor the low-frequency direct-commo bands."

"Yes, yes, Delta Vector. I'm sure you're picking up Pirate and Marauder chatter. No reason for alarm. Probably Van Allen belt echoes from that attack on our freighters last night. Those signals will be bouncing around the spectrum for a week at least."

"Yes, sir. I mean—no, sir! This isn't an echo. It's a voice, a strong voice. And it's singing."

"Singing? Delta Vector, did you say *singing?* Stay on the line, Delta." He switched lines. "Operational Control, this is supervisor control on the floor. I want a direct feed-line from Delta Vector."

And into his monitor minispeaker there came the static-distorted tones of a man's voice singing. "Won't you come home, Bill Bailey, won't you come home. . . ." The voice dropped the old song, switched over to businesslike, almost urgent tones. "Hey, you guys, wake up and fly right! What's goin' on there? I'm on final reentry countdown and I can't read anything from you. If I don't get some landing instructions from you, I'm going to put a big black hole right in the middle of beautiful downtown Burbank. Or Peoria. Or to tell the God's honest truth, I don't have the slightest idea of where the hell I'm heading!"

A look of puzzlement crossed the supervisor's face. "Practically a foreign language. Can it be some kind of joke?"

But the supervisor's thoughts weren't left to run their course. Another voice broke in, even more urgently, on the line. "Alert! Alert! Alien space craft invading defense belt, vector four one zero. Repeat, alien space craft. . . ."

The supervisor leaped into action. "My God!" he exclaimed, "it's heading directly for the defense shield!" Into his transmitter he almost shouted, "Get me intercept. Intercept squadron on the line—quickly! Top red-emergency!"

At Intercept Squadron headquarters the commanding officer picked up her handset. Colonel Wilma Deering was herself a beautiful woman, fully aware of her own features and the power they gave her in human dealings, but when she was on duty there was no consideration of glamour or romance. Her job was far too important for her to permit any dalliance to distract her from its performance.

"Colonel Deering here. Yes. I read. What are the coordinates? Right!" She hung her commo unit away, pressed the control stud under a glaringly flashing light. A raucous klaxon sent up its grating, grinding hoots. "Alert intercept!" Wilma commanded via loudspeaker. "Retard defense shield counterforce one hundred miles. Hold fire until we verify target identification!"

And from launching pads where sleek interceptor craft were held in flight-ready preparedness twenty-four hours a day, engines roared into shrieking, urgent life and gleaming, powerful fighting craft screamed away from earth, ready to engage any enemy that appeared.

"Alert intercept aircraft," Colonel Deering's voice came. "Stand by for readout on position of enemy craft!"

The War Room supervisor's voice came metallically over the transmitter to Wilma's earphone. "Very odd, Colonel."

"What's odd?" she snapped.

"Target seems to be moving unusually slowly for any known type of spacecraft. And its flight path is strange, too—erratic."

A technician's voice broke in on the line. "Target, thirty seconds from electronic destruct field."

Wilma Deering peered through her window. She was no deskbound commander, but flew every mission with her squadron, fought in every engagement and shared every risk that she asked her subordinates to run. "I have the target in visual sight, now," she was saying. "My God! What *is* that thing?"

As astonished as their commander, the members of the Intercept Squadron streaked past Buck's antiquated spaceship, banking smoothly for another pass at the intruder.

"All right," Buck Rogers exclaimed, unaware of the purpose of the craft that had scrambled to meet him. "Hey, really nice to see some friendly space-jockeys up to meet me!" His eyes widened, then narrowed again. "Wait a minute." He gazed in amazement at these sleek, yet brutally powerful space fighters as they roared around his primitive ship like turbohydroplanes circling a wallowing rowboat. "Who are you guys?" Buck asked weakly. "Hell, *what* are ya?"

The voice that returned through his headset was that of Wilma Deering. "Attention alien spacecraft. Do you read me?"

"You bet I read you! And watch who you're calling alien! You don't look so goddamned familiar yourself. Who are *you?*"

The female voice was sharp. "You will restrict your responses to yes and no. You are in grave danger."

"From who?" Buck demanded. "You?"

"You are traversing a narrow corridor into our inner cities."

"Inner what? Look, lady—"

"Colonel Deering, please. Commander, Intercept Squadron. Now please be quiet. If you deviate from my orders by so much as a thousand yards you will be burned into vapor. Do you understand that?"

"Vapor! Yeah, I got that. What do I do?"

"Do you have manual override capabilities?"

"You bet!"

"Then follow me very closely."

"I'll be right on your tail. Just show me the way, lady!" He punched the manual override button, putting his ship's computer into standby mode and taking control of the ship himself. *Just like an old-time jet jockey,* he thought to himself, and then— *well, we really blew it this time. That's gotta be the Russkies . . . that commander of theirs sounds like one tough chick!*

Through his speakers came the hard voice. "You're doing fine so far."

"Das vidanya," Buck replied bitterly.

"I beg your pardon?" the woman's voice sounded puzzled.

"Just being friendly."

"I didn't understand those last words. But let me assure you, whoever you are, pilot, that violating our planetary air space is not an act of friendship. It's an act of war!"

Buck shook his head and concentrated on following the sleek interceptor down to land. "Wait'll the guys at the Cape hear this one," he mumbled to himself. "Buck Rogers sets down right in the middle of Red Square. No question about it, they'll torture me for everything I know."

Minutes later he found himself seated inside a streamlined monorail car as it streaked along its track. It was surrounded by a city of incredible beauty, graceful towers and glistening spires thrusting upward nearly to touch the metallic and glassite dome that covered the entire metropolis.

Guards stood alertly at the front and rear of the monorail car. The only passengers between the watchful guardians were Buck Rogers and Wilma Deering. The car's windows were darkened, but he could peer through them and see the golden, glittering city outside.

"What is it?" Buck exclaimed. "This sure isn't the Moscow they told us about back in Chi Town!"

"This is the Inner City, of course," Wilma answered coldly.

"Inner City okay, but not just of course," Buck commented. "I've never seen anything like this. What kind of place is it?"

"Come away from the window, please," Wilma said. Although her words were couched as a request, their tone made it clear that she spoke a command. She pointed peremptorily to a button beneath the clear panel and Buck obediently pressed it. The window went dark.

49

"Look," he said, returning to his seat beside Wilma. "I think I deserve some kind of explanation. Where are we, really? I don't even know what planet I'm on!"

"What you undoubtedly deserve is a firing squad," Wilma answered sharply. "But we don't have those any more. We have a better fate awaiting you after your interrogation is completed."

"And I thought Princess Ardala was all a nightmare," Buck muttered bitterly.

"Princess Ardala!" Wilma jerked at the name. "I'm sure you'd like me to believe that she sent you. Well, it may interest you to know that whoever really did send you here planted a bomb on your ship. It was to be triggered by the earth's atmosphere entering your ship when you opened the hatch after you landed."

"A bomb?"

"Had we not moved your ship directly into a decontamination chamber to remove alien microbes, we would not have discovered the charge. And you, pilot, would be dead!"

Buck took a minute to assimilate this latest blockbuster. Not only was he no nearer to an understanding of what was taking place around him— each new revelation only seemed to move him farther away from one! He shook his head and stared introspectively into the darkened windowpanel. "If this is all a nightmare . . . then I can only say that it's a beaut!"

THREE

~~~~~~

A sterile room, gleaming white from floor to ceiling, from wall to wall. Light glared down from every direction. The room was furnished with the most spartan of implements. Two hard chairs. One small table. A single panel barely distinguishable from the sterile glaring walls that surrounded it.

And one living occupant.

William Rogers, Captain, United States Air Force.

Buck sat in one of the two chairs, gazing morosely at the white panel, wondering, wondering who or what might come through it—and when!

He stood up, moved away from his chair, strode nervously around the room chewing his lower lip, smacking the fist of one hand into the palm of the other. Finally he went to the white panel and tried to press it open. It did not respond.

Instead, an even more inconspicuous panel slid aside, at the opposite end of the room, and a man passed through it to stand staring at Buck from the rear. The newcomer was built along the delicate lines of a person who has lived long and grown far from the fleshly existence of youth or even middle age. His hair was a gray that was heavily salted with white. His features were thin, ascetic, almost spiritual in appearance. Yet a keenness of intellect so marked his features that no one would ever have mistaken him for less than the genius he was!

"Doctor Huer is my name," the newcomer announced. "I am very pleased to meet you, Captain Rogers."

Buck spun on one heel, faced the other in readiness to make any move necessary. "What in hell is going on here? Where am I and what are you doing to me?"

"We're studying you," Huer announced as calmly and matter-of-factly as if he were an adult answering the simple question of a small child.

Buck swung around, glaring at the walls and the ceiling of the sterile chamber.

"It's all electronic and quite painless," the old man told him. His voice was thin, his tone a strange combination of gentleness and abrasiveness, as if he had seen all that the world had to show, and had reached a point of tolerance toward human foibles, yielding only occasionally to impatience with the foolishness of the mortal beings.

"So far," Huer continued, "we're quite as astonished as you are, Captain, by what has happened. Your testing has provided the most phenomenal data!"

"All right, get to it," Buck snapped impatiently. "What's happened to me? If I'm dead, I obviously didn't make it to heaven. So just what planet is this?"

"What planet?" Huer laughed. "Why, Earth, of course! You returned yesterday morning, just as your mission required and on almost the precise landing area originally programmed into your ship's computer."

Buck shook his head despairingly. "Doctor, I may have been through a lot but there's no way you're going to tell me that city out there is anything like Chicago."

"No, it isn't," Huer conceded. "There's nothing like Chicago left on Earth. At least, nothing like the Chicago you knew in the twentieth century."

Buck stared speechlessly at the doctor.

"Captain," Huer resumed, "we're trying to find a way to ease you into what's happened."

Buck Rogers leaped from his chair and stood glaring at the tall scientist. "I was raised back in the 1960s, Doc. So don't be afraid to shock me. I know what culture shock is! Just let me have the facts, man! Tell me the plain truth and you can spare us both a lot of time and trouble beating around the bush!"

"I'm afraid that even I am not permitted to tell you everything," Huer replied. "For your own good, Captain, it's been decided that the shock would be too great—despite what you've just told me. Your 1960s were a difficult period, were they? I confess that my specialty is not ancient history."

"Never mind that. You say its been decided I can't handle the truth, hey? Well, *who* decided that? I have a right to—"

"Please!" the tall, lean scientist broke in. "I am but a humble man of science. Allow me to bring in my administrator, Dr. Theopolis."

"Aw, look, Doc," Buck complained in annoyance.

Huer crossed the wall to the semiconcealed white panel. It opened silently at his approach and he spoke to someone outside the sterile chamber. "Would you please bring Dr. Theopolis in here?"

From the opened panel there emerged the most astonishing creature that Buck Rogers had ever laid eyes on. In his own time there had been stories of intelligent robots, more or less manlike machines built with elaborate control circuitry capable of duplicating—or at least simulating—human thought. The famous ones—Adam Link, Helen O'Loy, R. Daneel Olivaw, Mr. Atom, Jay Score—had won their place in the hearts of lovers of extravagant literature.

But when the time came for the building of that

kind of creature, technology had taken a turn in a different direction. Instead of furnishing the ordinary household with a robot who would stand over a washtub by the hour, scrubbing dirty linens, the technologists had invented washing machines with their own controls to do the job. Later, instead of building humanlike robots and teaching them to fly airplanes, the technologists had invented autopilots and built them directly into the instrumentation of the planes. And so it had gone—the traditional, man-like robot of fancy and fiction from the Tin Woodsman onward, had been a scientific dead end, bypassed in the march of progress.

Or so it had been in Buck's day.

But now, there trotted into the sterile chamber a being whose very presence and existence disproved this theory of science. For here was a robot, made more or less along the lines of the fanciful ideas of Buck's own boyhood.

It was barely three feet tall, made in a humanlike but far from perfectly human form. It held its head at an angle and tottered around the room in a manner that brought Buck to the brink of laughter despite the desperate nature of his situation. For all that it was a thing of metal and glass, the robot reminded Buck of the caperings of a chimpanzee in the Chicago Zoo half a millenium before.

"What *is* it?" Buck asked Huer.

"Your drone," the scientist replied. "His name is Twiki."

"He's my—*what?*" Buck was flabbergasted.

While the two men spoke, the robot went about its business, totally ignoring them. It crossed the sterile chamber, opened another door and tottered into the next toom.

"For the duration of your debriefing and determination," Dr. Huer said, "he will act as your personal aide."

As Buck stood in gaping amazement, the drone tottered back into the sterile chamber and the door slid shut behind him. The robot was unchanged, but now he had an odd object hanging from a cable around his neck. The thing was not very large—smaller than a breadbox, Buck thought to himself, yet rather larger than a deck of playing cards.

It was clearly a highly sophisticated machine, with complex circuitry, controls and indicator lights that flashed continually, glowing brightly, dimming, flashing suddenly and then disappearing again. Yet—Buck wondered if it was his imagination at work or a real phenomenon he observed—the ever-changing pattern of lights bore an uncanny similarity to the features of a human face.

Then a voice came from the odd, boxlike object. It spoke not to Buck but to his scientist-companion, in a voice of astonishing richness, soft and benevolent, soothing and serene. Yet it was also a voice of absolute authority.

"Good morning, Doctor Theopolis," Huer greeted the box. "It's a lovely day."

"Thank you," the box replied. "I did my best today."

Buck gaped in amazement as the gray-headed scientist and the flashing lighted box conducted a pleasant social conversation. The scientist turned toward Buck and introduced the newcomer.

"Dr. Theopolis is a member of our Computer Council and in addition to his other duties, he is personally responsible for all environmental controls here within the Inner City."

The box said, "I'm introducing a pale hint of mauve into the sunset this evening. Not quite so deep as amethyst, but I'm trying for something more subtle, more of the texture of carefully roasted cinnamon."

The box's lights flashed with something that Buck Rogers had to identify as an expression of preening self-satisfaction.

"I do hope the Captain can watch it with us," Dr. Theopolis continued. "It's truly going to be lovely, and one does always strive to capture the approbation of a new audience."

Buck stared at the box, then murmured to Dr. Huer, "I'd do some checking if I were you. Find out who's programming that thing and maybe check *him* out a little."

The box indicated that it had heard every syllable. "Captain Rogers, it is we of the Council who do the programming for the entire city. Kindly reserve your opinions for your own delectation. Now," and the machine made a sound that can only be identified as clearing its throat, "shall we get down to cases?"

Dr. Huer rose and indicated that he was about to leave. "I shall offer you a little word of advice before I go, Captain Rogers. These drones, or quads as they are sometimes known, have been programmed by each other, over a span of many generations. We have been saved by them, in a sense. The mistakes that we made in areas like our environment have been entirely turned over to them.

"They averted what must have been certain doom for the earth, Captain. Little by little, they bring us back to where we will not have to depend entirely on other planets for food and water. A quad is not a human. But you *can* hurt their feelings—their circuitry and their programming include emotions. It is their sensitivity that separates them from mere machines."

Huer stepped through the doorway. As he disappeared he called back to Buck, "I'll see you in approximately sixteen hours."

"Sixteen hours!" Buck leaped to his feet. "Sixteen hours! Wait a minute!"

He started after Dr. Huer, jumped back just in time to avoid being clobbered by the automatically closing panel. "If you think I'm going to sit here talking to a package of Christmas lights for sixteen hours—"

"Sit down, Captain," the soothing voice of Dr. Theopolis came to Buck. "Now let's try to be as pleasant to each other as we can, eh? Please don't snap at me, and I shall try to be sympathetic to your plight. That's a good fellow. Thank you."

Buck stared at the box of flashing lights, dumbfounded.

Dr. Theopolis spoke to the quad from whose neck he hung. "Be a good drone, Twiki . . . and place me on the table where I can get a good look at the Captain. While Captain Rogers and I begin to get acquainted, perhaps you could offer him a bit of liquid refreshment."

"I don't need any refreshment!" Buck snapped.

"Of course you do," the soothing voice rolled on. "You're extremely dehydrated from your ordeal. Sit down, Buck—do you mind, may I call you Buck?"

While Buck stared, Twiki removed Dr. Theopolis from around his neck and placed him carefully on the table. The little robot marched mechanically through the sliding door.

"Well, now," the box of lights said, "what an attractive man you are, Buck. My word, are those eyes of yours *blue*?"

Buck slid slowly back into his chair. He felt as if he'd been handed a live concussion grenade and asked to make friends with it. "Blue," he murmured, "that's right."

"How truly rare blue eyes are these days," Dr. Theopolis said.

"My mother had blue eyes," Buck snapped back. "Look, can we blast right through this rainbow and get to it? I've been trying for twenty-four hours to find out where I am . . . *who* I am . . . who *you* are. . . . Can I please have some *answers?*"

"Certainly, Buck," the box of lights replied. "That's why I'm here. To answer your questions."

"Great! Then let's have it, the straight data!"

The lights flashed like a patient man nodding his head to calm an impatient adolescent. "First, you are Captain Buck Rogers. According to your ship's chronometer you left Earth in 1987 on a mission of exploration—"

"That much I know," Buck broke it. "Try telling me something I *don't* already know!"

"Well, if preliminary data hold up, it appears you have returned to Earth five hundred and four years later, to be precise. Buck—you, we, all of us —are now in the twenty-fifth century."

Buck stared at Theopolis, then turned to the drone Twiki who had returned and stood beside him with a glass in his metallic hand.

"I believe I will take that drink now, thanks. In fact, thanks very much!" He reached for the liquid and tilted back his head.

Elsewhere, in an efficiently furnished corridor, Dr. Huer was carrying on a consultation with Colonel Wilma Deering of the Intercept Squadron. They walked briskly along the corridor, almost trotting. Dr. Huer had just made a statement and Wilma Deering responded.

"I don't believe a word of it!"

"I'm not easily duped," Dr. Huer replied.

"It's not my opinion of you," the smartly uniformed officer said. "But my respect for those pirates who have been decimating my squadron. The pirates would do anything to prevent our completing a treaty with Draconia. Anything including planting a phony man-from-the-past on us, for heaven knows what purposes of espionage or sabotage."

While Dr. Huer and Colonel Deering continued their conference, Buck Rogers continued his confrontation with Dr. Theopolis. Still later, while Buck rested from his ordeal, the others met. The setting was a sleek, modernistic office, comfortable yet efficient. Dr. Theopolis rested on a desk between Colonel Wilma Deering and the gray-headed scientist Huer.

"You are wrong, Wilma," Theopolis's smooth voice poured from the box, "Buck Rogers is not a pirate or a plant of the pirates."

"It's Colonel Deering, not Wilma, to you, if you please." The officer was clearly not happy with the situation. "And I'll rely," she continued, "on the full Council's judgment, not yours alone."

"My dear," the box replied, "I personally interrogated Captain Rogers. You can take my word for it. He's a wonnnnnnnnnnnderful man, believe me!"

Wilma pursed her lips angrily. "I do believe you when you tell me you believe he's a wonderful man. But then, you're not being asked to risk the

61

lives of our few surviving warriors on sneaky subterfuge."

"He's only one man," Dr. Huer put in conciliatorily. "What could he possibly do to endanger our people?"

"He could attempt to discredit the treaty with Draconia!" Wilma snapped.

"But he has made no such attempt," Theopolis said. "He comes to us a very bewildered young man. Devastated by the loss of every loved one. To him, there is nothing left to save. He has already lost all."

"I would like an opportunity to spend some time with the captain," Wilma Deering said.

"If you're hoping to find fault with his testimony, you'll be wasting your time."

"Saving earth cannot be a waste of time, despite my having to endure the captain's company!"

"If Dr. Theopolis has no objections," Huer said, "*I* certainly have none."

"Then the captain belongs to me," Wilma asserted triumphantly, "until I expose him!" She rose from her seat and left the room, trailing a military sense of order.

The box on the desk said, "I've not seen Colonel Deering so uncharacteristically emotional about *anything* before this."

"About anything?" Huer echoed his mechanical colleague. "Or about *anyone*?"

* * *

On a downtown mall of the Inner City, golden elevators whisked silently up and down in transparent columns surrounding a central fountain of waters illuminated by dancing, colorful lights. Buildings and vehicles gleamed in a bright, pleasant light. Smartly dressed and happy citizens moved from place to place, stopping for a bit of refreshment, shopping, appreciating works of art that were carefully spaced around the plaza, or conducting any other business that they happened to have.

Far across the mall, dwarfed by the towering spire of levels of magnificent architecture, two figures strolled slowly, side by side.

The man gazed around himself, obviously awestruck by the magnificence of his amazing surroundings.

The woman, accustomed to the mall and everything in it, kept her attention for the man at her side.

"This part doesn't seem so much a nightmare as a beautiful dream," Buck Rogers commented happily.

"It's taken a long time to rebuild," Wilma Deering responded. "We've reached the point where we can once again start to grow. For more than four hundred years after the worldwide holocaust, people did little more than eke out their bare survival!"

"Tell me what happened," Buck almost pleaded. He was half-fearful to hear the horrors that he knew must be coming, yet he could not continue to live in this new world without finding out what had happened to the old one!

"I can't tell you," Wilma answered. "It isn't so much that I'm unwilling to tell you, it's the Council's decision. *They* will tell you, when they feel that the time has come to do so."

"I've been hearing that ever since I got here," Buck said angrily.

"Why is it so important?" Wilma demanded. "Why must you hear that story? The end of your world was so—ugly!"

Buck paused and reached for Wilma's hands. She let him take them. They stood facing each other, looking into each other's eyes. "I need to hear because until I do, until I hear it and feel it, it isn't real," Buck explained. "Look, I've lost everything I ever cared about. My father, mother, brothers and sisters. And—a woman who had sensitivities and feelings that make all you people seem like robots.

"You're sanitized, ethicized, scrubbed, polished, and packaged so completely that you don't realize you're acting like a pack of Pavlov's hounds. Your Computer Council rings the bell and everybody salivates, nice and neat and on command.

"But somewhere, somehow . . ." He stood gazing off, not into the gleaming vista of Inner City's plaza, but into the invisible mists of his lost past. "Someplace else in time and space, my own people, the real people, the real people are waiting for me. And until somebody shows me different, they're

64

going to remain more real to me than anything I've seen in this monument of plastic, or anyone I've met since I happened to doze off one afternoon in *Anno Domini* one-nine-eight-seven."

Buck and Wilma stood for long seconds, then the serious, almost bitter expression on his face gave way to a boyish look of abashment. "I guess that's the end of the tour. I'm sorry, Colonel Deering, that I don't make a better tourist here in your pretty plastic utopia."

He started to move away from her, but Wilma ran the few steps that separated them and put her hand on Buck's arm. "Wait! I'm sorry. I know it's hard for you to understand, but some of this is being done for your own good."

Buck suppressed a laugh. "Some of it?"

"There's our own security to think of. Look, give us a little time. We are a feeling people, whether we appear so to you or not. We *want* to trust you. But you'll have to put some of your trust in us, too. It can't be all one way, Buck."

He shrugged. "I don't guess I have a lot of choice."

She smiled. "No, I guess you don't either. But if you're ready to take it fatalistically, you *could* make things a little easier for us all, and a little pleasanter. How about a little glass of Vinol?"

He looked at her curiously. "A little glass of what?"

"It's a synthetic wine that we use. Some find it very intoxicating."

"Okay," Buck consented. "Then let's make it two or three. I'd like to get good and drunk."

They moved across the mall until they reached a pleasantly decorated area furnished with tables and chairs. The atmosphere was a little like that of a sidewalk cafe in the days of Buck's boyhood, but of course, here in the domed Inner City, there was no real difference between outdoors and indoors.

People were sitting at tables, sipping glasses of a shimmering liquid. Individuals and couples strolled up, greeted one another, forming and shifting into pairs and threesomes and quartets, then drifting away on other errands of their own.

Buck and Wilma found a vacant table and sat at it. A waiter appeared and Wilma ordered two Vinols.

As soon as the waiter had moved away to bring their drinks, Buck asked, "What's it like outside?"

"Outside the dome?" Wilma echoed. "You . . ." She considered for a little. "You wouldn't like it outside the dome."

"Why not? Too much radiation? Pollution? Environmental spoilage? We were making a mess of things back in my time. Some people were trying to preserve the countryside, but for every band of ecological idealists trying to save a wild river there were ten billion-dollar corporations swinging all their clouts to turn it into a running cesspool."

Wilma started to answer, but before she could speak Buck continued. "Or is it the opposite? Has the outside gone back to nature? Maybe there's a *real* utopia outside the dome and you people are afraid to let anyone see it for fear that they'll rebel against your shiny plastic world inside?"

Buck stopped speaking as the waiter arrived and placed drinks in front of each of them. As soon as the waiter had left, Wilma answered Buck.

"You're just being paranoid about a secret utopia outside and a conspiracy to keep the city people unaware of it. I wish that were the case! We could get past that in a breeze.

"No, I'm afraid that your first guess was more on target, Buck. There's radiation in some places, ruins and scorched earth just about everyplace else. That's why we're so dependent, now, on trade with other planets. We can't grow our own food here! We're trying to restore the earth, there are a few experimental farms and orchards under cultivation, but it's just the tiniest beginning."

"And this trade agreement," Buck said, "this treaty with Draconia. What's that all about? What's the role of this princess of theirs?"

"We're being starved out by pirates," Wilma said grimly.

"Star pirates! We had a look at star pirates five hundred years in advance. But nobody believed there would ever be such things really!"

"Well, there are! They've choked off our supply lines from our trading partners. The Draconians have promised to keep those supply lines open for us, in exchange for landing privileges here on earth."

"They aren't allowed to land now?" Buck asked.

"They're a powerful force, Buck. Frighteningly powerful. They've conquered worlds from here to Tau Ceti! We're afraid, frankly, of letting them have a toehold on our planet. But on the other hand, if we can get them to help us against the pirates, we can have an assured food supply until we've got our own production back to higher levels."

Buck shook his head. "If these Draconians are so powerful and Earth is in such a sorry state, why didn't they just swoop in here and take over?"

"We're very far from the strong-points of their empire. It would be very hard for them to wage war in Earth's sector. You have a military background, Captain Rogers. You understand about overextended lines of support."

Buck nodded to show that he did understand. "But if the Earth is such a mess," he countered, "if there's nothing growing here and the land is wrecked with radiation and rubble—why do the Draconians want to land at all?"

"Because Earth is the gateway to the galaxies beyond. I don't know how much was understood of cosmic astrogation in your time—"

"Damned little," Buck broke in. "We'd sent probes to the other planets and humans had visited the moon and worked in space. My own flight was to've been the first manned tour of the solar system, and I obviously didn't make it! What came after is a closed book to me! As of 1988 onward, you know more than I do, however much or little that might happen to be."

"Well," Wilma said, "I don't want to get too technical for starters, Buck. But speaking in layman's terms, space is like an ocean. You can travel across it, or through it—but there are reefs and shoals and whirlpools and all sorts of other perils. But there are also safe channels, and even shortcuts.

"And it so happens that, by reason of its location in the cosmic sea, Earth is a place of access to the farther island universes. I know my analogy to an ocean isn't perfect, but—"

"I understand," Buck nodded. "Yes, it makes sense, even to me." He grinned self-deprecatingly, just for a moment, before his features grew grim once again. "But what it amounts to, then, is that you're going to let the Draconians use Earth as a military base for conquering uncounted worlds,"— he gestured to the roof of the dome—"out there."

"The treaty has safeguards in it, Buck. It's for Earth's good."

"What kind of safeguards?"

"No man-of-war or ship bearing any kind of arms will ever be allowed within our defense shields. The only ships we'll let through are scientific exploration craft. And then, later on, trading vessels."

"That sounds nice. How do you think you can enforce it, once they're inside the shield?"

"That will be my job," Wilma said gravely. "My

job . . . ours . . . the military." Suddenly she changed the subject of their conversation. "You haven't even tasted your Vinol, Buck!"

He grinned at her and lifted his glass for a sip.

"Well, what do you think of it?" Wilma asked.

"It tastes—feminine," Buck commented.

"We're a culture of moderation," Wilma responded. "We don't go in for the tough, he-man kind of booze that you used to have back in your day."

"Huh! What do you do if you feel like being immoderate?"

"In our economy, Buck—why, things may look comfortable to you," she swept her hand in a circle, indicating the broad, shining mall. "But the truth is, everything is carefully balanced. We have little margin for error. None for waste. If somebody ruins a serving of food, or greedily consumes two when he's entitled to only one—then somebody else goes without a meal that day. That's how closely things are planned and balanced. What you would call immoderation, what you would call just a petty foible in your world—is a crime in mine. And criminals are invited to leave the Inner City."

"That's all?" Buck asked. "If they're criminals, aren't they jailed or punished in any other way?"

"The outside world isn't very pleasant any more. You said before that you thought there might be a secret utopia outside the domes. If you ever come to see the outside, you'll change your mind. The outside world has a name. Anarchia. There, you are denied the protection of society. You take your chances with thieves, murderers, and worse! Worse! Believe me!"

"You mean I'd risk all that just to get a stronger drink than this Vinol stuff?"

Wilma lifted her glass and they touched their rims before sipping again.

"To your treaty," Buck toasted.

Wilma said, "You seem unusually interested in that treaty for someone who claims no interest in it at all."

Buck shook his head. Their conversation seemed to bounce back and forth between lighthearted banter and deadly seriousness. "Something is bothering me about the treaty, yes," he conceded.

"Then you do have a point of view after all. Do you have something to recommend to the Council?"

"I'd like to see my ship," Buck said. "Is that possible?"

"Anything is possible," Wilma said. But there was suspicion in her face and doubt in her voice. "Anything is possible, Captain Rogers," she repeated.

FOUR

〜〜〜

Buck's five-hundred-year-old spaceship had been moved from its landing pad to a great, cavernous hangar. The distant walls of the place were so far off, so dimly illuminated that standing beside the ship gave one the impression of being in the center of a great, darkling plain, the spaceship and one-self the only objects for untold expanses in all directions.

Buck stood gazing thoughtfully at his old ship, Wilma Deering waiting at his side for some reaction.

"Those guards," Buck broke the silence. "They must have thought we were crazy coming out here at this hour of the night. But I admire the way you handled them, Wilma."

"Rank has its privileges, Buck. I *am* the commander of the Intercept Squadron, as well as carrying a full colonel's commission." She stifled a yawn. "The only crazy part of it for me, was having to wake up in the wee hours to get here!"

"You may not have had your usual beauty sleep," Buck said, "but I've had enough sleep to last me a lifetime. Five hundred years of shut-eye! I put old Rip Van Winkle to shame!"

He moved from Wilma's side and stood closer to his ship. He stood gazing wistfully inside, through its window, while Wilma watched him appraisingly. Suddenly Buck reacted to something he saw. He nearly jumped in surprise, then leaned over to examine some strange streaks that he found on the ship's fuselage.

He turned back toward Wilma, gestured urgently. "Can you identify these markings?" he asked.

Wilma moved to the ship, standing beside Buck. "Of course, in your day space exploration was just beginning and space war was something no one had ever experienced."

"Yes, so what?" Buck asked.

"Well, these streaks are fairly common on combat spacecraft."

"I wasn't in combat. The Draconians found me, revived me, and sent me back here to Earth. I remember when I was approaching, your craft came up and threatened me pretty effectively, but they didn't fire, did they?"

"Certainly not," Wilma asserted.

"Then—whose did? And—when?"

Wilma pondered. "Possibly the pirates who attack our shipping, took a few shots at you while you were having your long nap, Buck. You wouldn't have any memory of that happening, but you're lucky to be alive at all!"

He nodded in deep concentration. "Sure. But why didn't they finish me then? An inactive, derelict spaceship. If they didn't destroy me outright, they'd want to strip my spacecraft for salvage and loot, wouldn't they? Especially once I'd gotten their attention enough so they'd fired on me!"

"You were in space a long time," Wilma said. "Anything might have happened over those centuries."

Buck shook his head. "Not so," he disagreed. "Look." He rubbed his finger on one of the streaks, pulled it away and showed Wilma the vivid smudge on his flesh. "These burns are fresh! The cordite isn't even oxidized yet."

He gazed at the hangar floor in concentration, walked in a circle once while working out his thoughts. When he stopped he gazed straight into Wilma's eyes. "I think Princess Ardala's attack fighters fired on me before they towed my ship on board!"

"But that doesn't make sense either," Wilma exclaimed. "Princess Ardala's ship is unarmed. That's the law!"

"Then she's bending all hell out of it," Buck said angrily.

"If you're convinced of that, Captain, what do you suggest we do about it?'

"I'd search that royal space-barge or whatever you call that flying palace, before I'd ever let it inside Earth's defense shield!"

"That would be an insulting way to begin an alliance supposedly built up on good faith."

"Good faith is for diplomats," Buck answered bitterly. "And what it gets you is this," he gestured. "A plastic city with a dome on top of it and a ruined world outside. I'd go up there armed to the teeth. Full squadrons, fully prepared to fight. If I'm mistaken, you can always say it was a military escort of honor or some such line. Nobody'd *really* be fooled, but it would save face all around. But if you don't, you're just sitting ducks!"

Wilma said, "For a man who's been asleep for five hundred years, you seem to have strong opinions about this world you never made."

"Yeah," Buck grated. "You're absolutely right. It's none of my goddamned business how you blow up your world. My generation didn't understand what the hell we were doing either, and it looks like we knocked it all apart shortly after I crawled into my jammies, so I guess there's a kind of rough justice there after all. Well, thanks for everything, Colonel. Go back to bed and sweet dreams to you."

He turned and began to stride away, across the floor of the vast, echoing hangar.

"Just a minute, Rogers! Where do you think

you're going?" Wilma Deering was all the military commander now.

Buck stopped and turned back toward her for a moment. "I'm going outside the city, thanks."

Wilma started to run after him. "You can't do that," she cried in horror. "It's—you'll die out there, Buck!"

"I've got to find out what happened to my people," he said.

"That's forbidden!"

"You're joking! This is a free country, Colonel. Or at least it used to be."

"Captain Rogers, you are in a technical state of military custody. Regardless of what we think of each other, you're officially my prisoner and I'm officially your guard. I cannot let you escape."

"You can't stop me."

She put her hand on the holster attached to her military officer's tunic. "I can, Buck. Don't make me."

Buck walked away from her, advancing steadily toward the exit from the hangar. It was a calculated risk, he knew. In his life he had faced down many deadly foes, from enemy pilots in combat fights, to cold-blooded murderers to raging berserkers. He knew that the first few seconds were the most critical.

He knew that Colonel Wilma Deering, despite her military position, was a warm, feeling human being. Even as he had accused her entire world—and by implication Wilma herself—of being an army of emotionless, conditioned zombies, her own reactions had shown the anger and distress that he had provoked. He knew that she would balk at the prospect of shooting him now.

There was no question of her courage. She could face up to an opponent in fair battle and give as good as she got—could kill without hesitation in a kill-or-be-killed confrontation. If she had been incapable of that, she would never have reached the position of command she now occupied. She would have transferred to a softer branch of service long ago, or paid for her bravado with her life.

But would she shoot a man in the back?

An unarmed man?

Buck knew that *Colonel* Deering's sense of duty required her to undog her holster, open its flap, lift her sidearm from it, aim at him and fire if he refused to stop. But he knew that *Wilma* Deering's sense of humanity and fair play would do battle with her sense of duty. And if the two countering impulses held her paralyzed for a few seconds more he would be out of her sight, into the dark shadows that ringed the edges of the cavernous hangar. In another ten seconds or so, he calculated, he would be into the shadows, invisible to even Wilma Deering's sharp eyes—and safe.

He counted down—ten . . . a couple of paces . . . nine . . . a couple more . . . eight . . . and he heard a slight sound behind him . . . seven . . . he fought down an impulse to look over his shoulder, an impulse that would reestablish eye-contact between himself and Wilma, an impulse that might be fatal . . . six . . . five . . . he thought he heard a soft sob from behind him, and felt himself tremble as he continued to walk purposefully ahead . . . four . . . he was past the halfway mark in his march from peril to safety . . . three . . . he could all but *feel* the shadows deepening around him . . . two——and the world ended!

Buck never knew what hit him. There was no sound of an explosion of propellent fuel or discharge of electrical potential; there was no sense of impact, no flash, no odor of burned cordite or sour, ionized ozone.

There was just—nothing.

Wilma Deering stood dumbly where she had stood to fire her sidearm at the escaping prisoner. She had seen the flash of her hand-laser, felt the surge of electricity as it went screaming through every atom in Buck Rogers's body. For the seconds that she hesitated she had been two women.

Colonel Deering of the Intercept Squadron coldly and deliberately performing her duty to the service and her planet. And she had been Wilma Deering, woman of flesh and blood and emotions, struggling to keep her other self from firing at the man for whom she had come to feel as she had never before felt for any other person.

And now, the dutiful military officer having triumphed for just the length of time it took to raise and fire her weapon, the warm, feeling woman stood shattered by her own cold-blooded act.

She lowered the laser, dumbly returned it to its holster and stood watching the scene before her. She saw guards rushing from the remote entrances of the hangar toward the motionless form of the man she had shot.

A day later Dr. Huer looked up from his desk at the sound of the door to his office opening. A box stood on his desk, its surfaces gleaming translucent plexiglass through which multi-colored lights flashed and glowed in an ever-changing, yet oddly facelike pattern. Between the aged scientist and the computer-brain lay a typewritten document both had been studying.

Colonel Wilma Deering entered the office and stood for a moment contemplating the scientist and the computer-brain. Her glance finally took in the document and she asked them what it might be.

Huer cleared his throat as if to win a delay of even half a second in answering the young woman. Then he said, "It's something to make you feel a little better about what you had to do last night." He lifted the paper from the desktop and handed it to Colonel Deering.

She stood silently while she scanned its contents, then read it a second time, more carefully. At last she raised her eyes from the flimsy sheet to the face of the old scientist. "Then it's true," she said despairingly, "he was working for the pirates."

Before Dr. Huer could answer her words the computer-brain on his desk flashed its lights into a brighter pattern than ever. "I don't agree with you," the computer grated, "I simply am not convinced of Rogers's guilt."

Dr. Huer raised his hands in resignation. "You're entitled to your opinion, of course, just like anyone else, Theo. But you see, you'll find yourself standing alone, if you'll pardon my use of the expression. The evidence is conclusive, isn't it?

"Rogers's ship had a microtransmitter attached to its navigational computer. Whoever had a receiver tuned to the transmitter's frequency now has a nice clear map revealing all of earth's secret access corridors through space. . . ."

"Still . . ." The computer-brain was hesitant to accept Huer's conclusions.

"Still indeed," the old man said. "Our planet is in the soup now. Who do you think was on the other end of the circuit, Theo? I think it was the pirates, and now we're more dependent upon the protection of the Draconian Empire than ever. And as for Captain Rogers, I think he stands convicted by his own actions. Coming in here with that mapping transmitter in his ship, then trying to escape from the custody of Colonel Deering. . . ."

He shifted his glance from the computer to the colonel as he mentioned her name. He saw her turn away, unbelieving, stunned by the new, damning evidence against the man she was still hoping to see vindicated. "At first I thought he was guilty," Wilma sobbed. "But then—" She was unable to continue.

"Personal contact is always a mistake, my dear." That came in the computer voice of Dr. Theopolis.

Wilma wheeled furiously upon the box of lights. "Don't lecture me on human behavior, Doctor. I may not be the world's greatest expert on the subject, but I believe I have an edge on you!"

"I meant nothing personal," the computer said. "But you are obviously being subjective in the way your evaluation is made. I, on the other hand, also support Buck Rogers. But for very practical and impersonal reasons."

"What are they?" Dr. Huer asked.

"Well," Theopolis replied, "I am convinced of one thing. Our friend Captain Rogers has indeed met Princess Ardala and been aboard the Draconian flagship. His descriptions are too precise to be the guesswork of a pirate."

Gaining hope, Wilma said, "Maybe the pirates have been aboard Princess Ardala's ship. They could have coached Buck. . . ."

"My dear," Theopolis said, "they are the deadliest of enemies. It is unlikely that any pirate could survive such a visit at all."

"Then you think the Council will share your

faith in Captain Rogers? Even in the face of this damning evidence?"

"Of course they will. I am a member of the Council, revered and respected by all."

Theopolis's lights flashed smugly.

In deep space, far above the entry corridors to earth, the Princess Ardala's Draconian flagship still drove contemptuously through the blackness. Its every line, every jet-thruster, every jutting laser-weapon spoke of its arrogance and strength.

In the private quarters of the Princess Ardala, the mutant Tigerman who stood constantly on guard moved aside grudgingly and permitted the Princess's caller to enter.

The visitor was Kane.

"Word from earth," Kane announced.

The Princess Ardala was in her luxurious bath, surrounded by a group of ladies in waiting. They themselves were only half-clad, as they performed their duties of attending to every luxurious whim of their mistress, anointing her smooth skin and gleaming sensuous tresses with exotic oils and fabulous perfumes.

Kane pointedly ignored the display of feminine allure that paraded before his hungry eyes. "Word of Captain Rogers's fate," he elaborated.

Now the Princess Ardala looked up, deeply interested. "He's alive," she told Kane.

"How did you know that?" he demanded, his eyes narrowing coldly.

"I knew," Ardala replied mysteriously.

"Well, you're right! His ship was intercepted and led down to planetfall, as I expected."

"And did the transmitter we secreted aboard the ship, provide the information we need? Can we lead father's forces through Earth's defense shield now?"

Kane looked uncomfortable. "Well, yes, I suppose so."

"You suppose so?" the princess snapped furiously. "What do you mean, you suppose so? I want a straight answer to my questions, Kane, not an evasion."

"The transmitter has been discovered, my princess. So—we know the present pathway through their shielding, but they know that their shield has been compromised. By the time we could get the Imperial fleet to Earth, they'll surely have changed the coding and we'll be back in a standoff again."

"Then we cannot win," Ardala gritted furiously.

"Oh, no," Kane shook his head. "Not so, my Princess, not so at all! We cannot lose! We will enter their shield in the guise of a peaceful diplomatic trade mission, and once they have welcomed us inside, we will destroy the entire shield from within and extend a welcome to the Imperial fleet!"

The princess smiled grimly. "So. You would destroy their defenses from within. Just as you destroyed Buck Rogers. Kane, I thought you were going to plant a bomb on Rogers's ship."

"I did, my Princess. But Rogers eluded it."

Ardala smiled enigmatically. "Poor Kane. Outwitted . . . by a five-hundred-year-old man."

Kane's face assumed a petulant, bitter expression. "Don't you worry," he asserted, "Captain Rogers is as good as dead. He will not be able to explain the presence of the microtransmitter in his ship's computer circuitry. They'll know who betrayed their defenses. In fact, they know it already." Kane grinned wolfishly. "At this very moment, Buck Rogers is on trial for his life!"

In a comfortable but spartanly furnished waiting room in the heart of the Inner City on Earth, Buck Rogers sat on a sofa, his head held despairingly in his hands. Beside him the quad Twiki stood patiently, the computer-brain Dr. Theopolis draped again around his metal neck.

Theopolis's voice was at its richest and most sympathetic as the computer-sage asked Buck how he felt. The very lights of Dr. Theopolis seemed to blink in kindly concern.

"I feel terrible," Buck moaned. "What did she use on me?"

"A laser charge set to stun," Theopolis replied. "No question about it, Buck, women just don't seem to take to you."

"Women?" Buck raised his face from his hands and stared at the light-face curiously. "What do you mean by that?"

"Let's face it," Theo answered. "Princess Ardala

84

tried to plant a bomb under you, Wilma Deering shot you with her laser. . . ."

"I guess I'm just out of step with the times."

"Well, I'm going to get you back in, Captain. Now stop worrying about this little trial. I'm a member of the Council and I am going to defend you personally."

"It's nice to have at least one friend," Buck muttered.

Suddenly the robot drone Twiki cocked his head at an odd angle and gave off a shrill, hurt squeal.

"Sorry, Twiki," Buck laughed. "Two friends."

That was the last laugh that Buck had before he was led into the darkened Council Chamber for his trial. It was a good thing that he had it, for the trial itself was as grim and deadly an ordeal as ever accused man had had to endure.

The Chamber was as dark as the darkest chamber of the now almost legendary Inquisition of medieval times, with only a single oval window positioned as if to torment the victim with a final glance of the world of light and life and color that he had forever forfeited by whatever crime brought him before the Council.

A dark, semicircular table filled most of the room, and placed at equidistant positions around its perimeter stood eleven boxes, each containing circuits and indicator lights that bore an uncanny resemblance to eleven grave counsellors gathered in mortal debate. Behind each of the eleven, stood a motionless, gleaming, three-foot-tall robot-drone, ready to take decisive action as soon as the Council so directed.

A cold, mechanical, computer-created voice rang throughout the silent Council Chamber. "The Computer Council is ready now to hear final arguments in the case of the Directorate versus Captain Buck Rogers . . . on charges of espionage, and of treason." There was a moment of silence, then the voice spoke once more. "We will hear now from Counsellor Apol."

The glowing lights on the face of one of the computer-boxes increased in intensity, as a spotlight mounted in the ceiling of the Chamber also shone down upon the computer. The Council had been in long session, but the computers and their drone-servants knew no fatigue. Counsellor Apol presented the summary of the prosecution case in his mechanically grating voice.

"The state's case is elementary," Apol grated. "Captain Rogers piloted a foreign aircraft through our defense network on a path that could only have been programmed by a hostile force in possession of secret information available only to this Council and a handful of key military personnel.

"His explanation of this situation, while stopping just short of the physically impossible, is totally lacking in credibility. He has been unable to provide us with a single shred of evidence to prove that he is a son of this planet and not the off-spring of some long-forsaken outcasts!

"What price, you may ask, what bounty, would Captain Rogers consider his just reward for selling out the human race and the planet Earth? Only his pirate friends can answer that, but I will offer my fellow Counsellors an educated guess. I suggest that the price of treason is the destruction of Earth's treaty with Draconia. The pirates seek this at all costs! For its enactment spells doom for them!"

There was a long, dramatic pause, then Apol stated simply, "The prosecution rests its case."

The ceiling light dimmed over Apol, as the lights on the front of his control panel slowly returned to their normal, semihumanoid form.

Now the light grew in intensity over another computer-box, and the great impersonal voice of the Council said, "Theopolis, we will now hear from the defense."

For a moment Buck Rogers, silently witnessing the proceeding upon whose outcome his future and his very life hung by a thread, shifted his gaze to the oval window of the Chamber. Through the glass he could see the witnesses of the trial: an array of civil authorities and military dignitaries, and a few interested parties including a grim-faced Wilma Deering and the gray-headed, tall genius Dr. Huer.

Buck's attention was recaptured by the voice of

Dr. Theopolis. "Distinguished colleagues," the computer said, "you have heard the evidence, and on its strength I challenge you to find Buck Rogers guilty!"

Buck gaped incredulously at Theopolis as he issued the challenge, and at the other ten Counsellors as they received it.

"No evidence," Theopolis continued, "has been produced to support a claim to Rogers's birth upon this planet because—as we all know fully well—no records survived the great holocaust. Captain Rogers has no explanation as to how his ship was programmed to maneuver through our defense shield," he paused dramatically, then resumed, "because," another momentary pause, "*it . . . was . . . not . . . his . . . doing!*"

There was another pause while Theopolis let his summary of the defense sink into the other ten members of the Computer Council. "Buck Rogers is an innocent pawn in the great war," Theopolis concluded, "but I go on record as testifying that this man can be one of our truly great leaders. That destiny has placed him here amongst us now, to help deliver us from our enemies."

With a bitter, ringing irony, Apol countered: "From our enemies, Theopolis? Or *to* our enemies?"

"No," Theopolis blinked his lights as a human would shake his head. "No, Apol. No, I say to you, to all my colleagues here, that if you find this man guilty, you must find me guilty as well. For

I cannot continue to serve a society that doubts the core of my being. I am programmed to be discerning. My sensors tell me that this man is good."

Now the disembodied voice of the Computer Council spoke again. "Captain Rogers—have you any last words before we pass judgment?"

Buck rose slowly from his seat. He seemed to be speaking to the disembodied voice rather than to Theopolis or Apol or any other of the members of the Council. Through the oval window Wilma and Dr. Huer could be seen inching forward, balancing on the edges of their chairs.

"I'd just like to say this," Buck began, "I don't blame you for lining up against me. Someone—or something—is selling you out. I didn't find my way through your shield. Someone pulled the strings to arrange all of that. But you'd be better off worrying less about me, whatever happens to me personally, and worrying more about whoever or whatever it was that did that string-pulling. I can't do you any more harm, even if I were guilty of the charges against me. That damage is done. But the one who engineered all of this can still do harm. He can destroy you, in fact!" Buck finished his statement to the Council, looked around the room once more, and resumed his chair.

The lights on Dr. Theopolis's control panel flashed brightly. "Very nice work, Buck. We don't have a thing to worry about!"

There was a momentary pause while the eleven computers of the Council were electronically polled as to their verdicts, then the great voice spoke once more. "By unanimous vote, the Council finds for the state. Captain Rogers, you and your representative, Counsellor Theopolis, are banished from the Inner Cities. You will be removed at once to Anarchia, there to live out your lives as you see fit.

"This Council is adjourned."

If ever a computer could be said to gasp in astonishment, Dr. Theopolis did so when he heard the verdict of the Council. "I don't believe it!" his mellow voice sounded completely disconcerted.

On the other side of the oval window of the Council Chamber, bureaucrats and military officers were shaking hands and clapping one another on the back in congratulation at what was obviously a highly popular verdict. Justice was no concern of theirs. They were part of the official *status quo* of the Inner City; the established order of things had been challenged by the very appearance of this unruly man-from-the-past. Now he was to be disposed of, the powers-that-be could return to their usual state of tranquility, and all was rejoicing among the ruling circles.

Only two individuals in the spectators' room failed to join in the general celebration. One was Colonel Wilma Deering of the Intercept Squadron; the other, Dr. Huer, the sage of the Inner City. Dr. Huer had risen and started for the door at the moment that the verdict was announced. Now he turned back to face the spectators and spoke to one of them.

"Wilma, are you coming, child? We've got a lot to do, a lot of preparations to make for the Princess Ardala's escort down to Earth from orbit."

Stunned, almost as if sleep-walking, Wilma assented. "Yes, Dr. Huer," she said, "I—I'm coming, Doctor."

She tossed a last glance behind her, over one shapely tunicked shoulder. "Funny," she said, almost to herself, "in a way Buck is just getting what he wanted all along. He just doesn't understand what's going to happen to him when he gets there."

On the other side of the glass, Buck Rogers calmly submitted to the guards who flanked and escorted himself and Twiki—the quad with Dr. Theopolis hung around his neck—from the room.

It was barely a matter of an hour before two lonely forms plodded down the road from the Inner City to the barren and seething land of Anarchia. One was Buck Rogers; the other, Twiki with Dr. Theopolis hung from his neck.

They stopped in the middle of the road, for there was no traffic here to prevent their doing it, and stood, gazing back at the great glowing dome of the Inner City.

"I never thought I'd say this," Buck muttered, "but that place is starting to look good to me!"

The little quad made one of his infrequent little squawks of distress. Dr. Theopolis, hanging from the drone's metal neck, glowed softly as he spoke. "I wouldn't start feeling sorry for myself yet, Twiki. This is nothing compared to what lies ahead of us."

"Maybe we ought to stay right here until it gets light," Buck suggested.

"Oh, I'm afraid we'd freeze to death," Dr. Theopolis said. "That is, you would freeze to death, Buck. But in fact, it wouldn't be any too good for Twiki's mechanical fittings or for my own more environmentally sensitive circuits. It'll be way below zero here long before sunrise starts it to warming up again."

Buck shrugged, and he and Twiki turned away from the Inner City and began their slow walk along the windblown road.

"Well," Theopolis philosophized, "I guess we just have to move on, then."

"I'm sorry," Buck said. "I did what I believe was right, and for my own sake I'd do it again if I had to. But I'm sorry that I had to take you fellows down with me."

"No one forced me into your camp," Theopolis replied. "I did what I did because I believed in you, Buck. And I still do—and I'd do it again if I had to, as well!"

Buck thanked the computer.

The drone Twiki made an odd squeaking sound.

"What'd he say?" Buck asked Theopolis.

"You don't want to know," the computer replied.

And they kept walking, kept walking, up the windswept road, away from the brilliant domed city, and towards the vague and distant outline of ruin and desolation.

FIVE

Back in the Inner City, in the office of Dr. Huer, to be specific, the old scientist was sitting, disconsolately contemplating the recently completed trial and its tragic verdict. He looked up in surprise as Wilma Deering hurriedly entered and cried out to him, "Doctor, I need your help—desperately!"

"What is it?" Huer asked, startled.

"It's Buck Rogers." Wilma was nearly in tears. "We must get him back, Dr. Huer, we must!"

"Back? My dear," the old man said, "you can't be serious. You know what the life expectancy is outside the Inner City?"

"It's the life expectancy of the Inner City itself that I'm concerned with saving, Dr. Huer. That, and the entire planet Earth!"

Huer's eyebrows flew ceilingward in alarm. "What are you saying, child?"

"I realize now how foolish I was in pressing for the Council to pass judgment on Captain Rogers. We had the perfect test of his guilt or innocence in our hands, and we failed to apply it!"

Dr. Huer shook his head in puzzlement. "I'm afraid I don't—"

Wilma interrupted the old man. "Buck Rogers claims that the Draconians helped him. He could provide us with the perfect opportunity, the perfect *excuse*, to go aboard their ship and check out his story."

"While using the same expedition to do a little looking around for—other things. That is very good, child."

"Exactly," Wilma agreed. "It's a good plan, I have to say that even though I invented it myself."

"Well," old Huer said drily, "you chose a fine time to think of it. I doubt that Captain Rogers feels in a very friendly or cooperative mood as far as the Inner City is concerned. That is, if he's even alive."

"Never mind," Wilma cried. "I know he's alive, somehow. Just help me to convince the Council to suspend their sentence while they review my new findings."

Huer rubbed his chin with a pale, blue-veined hand. "I'll try, Wilma, that's all that I can promise you. I'll try."

* * *

In the Council Chamber of the Computer Council of the Inner City, membership had been brought back to a full twelve by the elevation of a replacement for the banished Dr. Theopolis. The Counsellors were again assembled, the lights dimmed, and this time it was not Buck Rogers but Dr. Huer who held the floor of the meeting.

"It is in the city's and planet's best interests," Dr. Huer was saying. "As things stand now, we have nothing further to lose, for all will be lost anyway."

"But the very fabric of our society," the computer Apol said, "is threatened when a ruling of the Council is reversed, or even suspended. The word of the council must be final and absolute."

"No," Huer differed. "This case transcends all rules and precedents of the Council. If the Council has erred in its judgment, the danger of letting the error stand is far greater than that of admitting fallibility and correcting the error. If by some horrible error of judgment the Draconians are admitted to Earth, and they come to us not as friends but as traitors and enemies in our very midst— *then* will all be lost! Then we would suffer an absolute defeat. Therefore we *must* seize this opportunity to verify the honesty of their stated intentions."

The disembodied voice of the Council rang out. "You make a good case, Dr. Huer."

"But a dangerous one," the computer Apol differed. "The Draconians are the most powerful force in all the civilized universe, and if they are insulted by our behaviour, we will be in dire peril."

The disembodied voice replied loudly. "They can only be sympathetic to our need to find justice in the case of this man who has suffered at our hands, and who has offered the Draconians' own charity as his only defense."

"Nonetheless," the computer Apol shrilled petulantly, "nonetheless, nonetheless, learned Counsellors, I wish to go on record, yes to go on record, as being opposed to this motion. Opposed, yes, opposed to this motion." His lights blinked furiously until it appeared that he was in danger of blowing a circuit.

"Are there any others in opposition?" the great voice asked calmly. When no others joined Apol, the voice resumed. "Council moves to suspend Captain Rogers's sentence until it, and the evidence upon which his conviction was based, have been reviewed."

In the spectators' room Dr. Huer turned to Wilma. She ran and hugged him in jubilation. "Thank you, Doctor. You were wonderful!"

Dr. Huer's answering glance was sober. "I'm afraid that this action by the Council means nothing if you can't locate Captain Rogers in time!"

"We'll find him in time," Wilma answered gravely, "we'll find Buck!"

"I'd like to go with you, my dear. I'd like to

help if I could, but—" He gestured as if to say, *the spirit is willing but the flesh is too old.* "But you must take a sizeable force," he resumed. "You know that the sight of Inner City troops rouses the mutants and their rabble companions to a rage. You'll need a strong party to stand off their attack."

"I'll have no trouble finding volunteers," Wilma said. "For some reason, the members of the Intercept Squadron seem to regard Captain Rogers as some sort of folk hero. We'll have to leave behind a crew to man duty stations, but every member of the squadron who can be spared, will almost certainly want to go."

Huer smiled sadly, disappointed at having to pass up the adventure of rescuing Buck. "Try to keep him from becoming a martyr as well," he said. "Good luck to you, Wilma. Good luck to you all."

He reached for her hand before she spun around to leave, but as he did so Wilma impulsively leaned over and kissed the old man on the cheek. He raised his hand to the spot her lips had touched and gazed wistfully after her as she strode away.

Striding side-by-side down the windswept road, Buck and Twiki with Theopolis suspended from his neck had reached the remnants of a ruined city. This was the true heart of Anarchia: craters, rubble, bricks and girders and shards of glass lying higgledy-piggledy where they had tumbled in that last paroxysm of combat between the forces of old America and her enemies.

No vehicle moved in the cracked streets; instead, rank weeds had sprouted in every crevice and spread their sickly effluvium over the macadam. Vicious rats, skulking mongrel hounds, giant aggressive insects scuttled from shelter to hole. Some of the shadows contained vague, dark, ragged figures that might have been humans or the descendants of humans; their uncertain forms held a promise of horror indescribable, and the reality of their faces and bodies more than fulfilled the worst substance of that promise.

As Buck and the drone advanced warily from their wilderness into this living hell, the quad exclaimed in his wordlessly eloquent squeal and the computer hung around his neck flashed in horror. "Oh, my word," Theopolis crooned, "oh, heavens preserve us! I knew that Anarchia would be bad, but this is worse than ever I'd even imagined."

"Just keep moving," Buck urged huskily.

Again Twiki made his squeaking noise. "What's he saying?" Buck demanded of Theopolis.

"You don't want to know," the computer answered.

"Stop saying I don't want to know. I *want* to know!"

"Very well, Buck, but don't say I didn't warn you. Twiki says he thinks we're being followed."

Buck swung around to check on the little

drone's suspicions. A darkened, wrecked doorway stood nearby, leading into the hulk of what once had been a building of some size. In the murky dusk a group of horrific shadows seemed to duck into the doorway.

"Just your imagination," Buck said to the drone. "Come on Twiki, let's just keep moving ahead."

The drone squeaked again.

"Twiki says he doesn't believe you," Theopolis interpreted.

"Tell him he's a lot smarter than I thought," Buck conceded. "But come on anyhow. There's no point in playing target for some half-human bird of prey!"

With Buck in the lead, they slipped down a side street, found their way into a shadowed opening not unlike the one from which they had been menaced. On the street they had deserted, a group of shapes emerged from the building-hulk. There were five of them, and for all their indistinction they could all be identified as human—after a fashion.

They hobbled and scuttered down the street after Buck and Twiki and Theopolis, muttering and mumbling horrifying parodies of human speech as they went.

Theopolis somehow sensed their presence. "My God!" he cried.

"Shhh!" Buck warned. Then, in a whispered undertone, "What do you mean, your God? Who made you anyhow, somebody down at the canning works?"

"This is no time to discuss theology," Theopolis whispered back to Buck. "Oh, my God, this situation is hopeless, absolutely hopeless. Oh, why didn't we stay out in the countryside where all that was going to happen to us was that we'd freeze to death!"

"We'll be all right," Buck insisted. "Don't throw in the sponge now, Theopolis."

"What sponge? Oh, you always use those strange expressions, Rogers. But I do have a little cheering news, I think."

"I could sure use some," Buck sighed. "What is it, computer old pal?"

"It isn't you that they're after. Those mutants, I mean."

"What?" Buck asked, astonished.

"Well, I suppose they could make *some* use of you." Theopolis murmured something softly to his drone and Twiki raised a metallic arm and prodded Buck appraisingly in the side. The quad squeaked something to the computer. "Yes," Theopolis continued, "I agree with Twiki. You're still young enough to be tender, Buck. A trifle too muscular to make really choice merchandise, but at least you're not all old and stringy like Dr. Huer would be. He'd never be worth a plugged nickel on the black market. But you'd draw a fair price, yes." He flashed his lights for a while.

"You mean they're cannibals, eh?"

"Only as a sideline, Buck. As I was saying, they're not *really* interested in you, although if they had occasion to bash your skull in with a rock they wouldn't want to let you go to waste, that's all. But they're much more interested in Twiki. And—I blush to say this—myself." At the expression about blushing, Theopolis's lights glowed an embarrassed crimson.

"They want you?" Buck stared at the little quad and the computer around his neck. "For what? Advice?"

"Now don't be flippant!" the computer answered petulantly. "The fact is, many of my circuits contain precious metals. Gold, iridium, platinum. To me they're precious because I do my thinking with them. But to *them*," and he emphasized the word with a scornful tone, "they're just precious metals that they can sell, or barter for food or tools."

Buck nodded and said, "Ah, hah!"

"As for Twiki," Dr. Theopolis went on, "I hate to tell you the purposes they would have for him. Poor creature. You know, quads don't have anywhere near the grade of computer-brain that we Counsellors have. They're designed to be docile little servants, and they're very good at that, but that doesn't mean that they're just *things*."

Twiki squealed.

"No, of course you're not just a thing," Theopolis said soothingly. "You have a mind and you have your feelings, Twiki, as I was just explaining to Buck here. Everyone knows that, Twiki."

The quad squealed again, a more mollified sound than his previous complaining tone.

"And if those mutants should ever get hold of poor Twiki," Theopolis rambled on. Suddenly he stopped. He'd become so engrossed in his own monolog and in the quad's reactions to it that he had failed to notice when Buck disappeared.

Theopolis murmured frantically to Twiki. The drone scuttered out of their protective doorway, into the middle of the street, twisting and scanning the street, using his mechanical joints to direct his optical sensing devices one way and then another, until he located Buck at last.

Twiki gave a squeal of relief. Buck was only a moderate distance away from them, standing before a half-demolished building and staring at the lettering carved into its concrete.

"How do you like that," Theopolis grumbled, "I confide our predicament to the man-from-the-past, and instead of trying to help us escape he drops us like a hot rock."

Twiki squealed indignantly in agreement.

"Well, you're absolutely right, my dear drone," Theopolis resumed. "He got us into this, not we him. And he'll just have to devise a way of getting us out of it."

With Dr. Theopolis still hanging around his neck, Twiki scuttered across the shattered pavement after Buck. From behind the astronaut, the computer and the drone could see the lettering on the building that Buck was staring at.

It was simply an old street marker, designed to let people know the name of the thoroughfare that ran in front of the building. It said, *State Street*.

Twiki moved around in front of Buck and looked up at the man. From around the drone's neck, the computer-brain spoke. "I don't mean to impugn your strategy, Buck . . . but standing in the middle of the street is hardly wise under the circumstances, do you think?"

As if he hadn't heard a syllable of the computer's words, Buck strode distractedly around the corner of the building to look at it and the cross-street from another angle. Curiously, Twiki and Dr. Theopolis followed.

More to himself than to the others, Buck mumbled, "I can't believe it. I just can't believe it."

The lettering on this side of the old concrete cornerstone said, *Michigan Avenue*.

Buck swung around, faced the others and commanded, "Come on!"

To the astonishment of Twiki and Theopolis, Buck Rogers sprang away at a dead run. The five-hundred-year layoff had not softened his tendons or cut into his wind. He set a fast but steady pace that the little quad was hard-pressed to match, even with the power and speed of his mechanical undercarriage to give him the advantage.

"Saints preserve us," Theopolis exclaimed, "he's found a way out of Anarchia!"

Buck pounded up one street and down another, obviously on familiar territory. If the truth be known, he was indeed on familiar territory. Although he had not set foot on these streets for half a millenium, he knew them as thoroughly as a blind man knows the inside of his own house. He could have made his way through this maze of thoroughfares blindfolded without missing a stride —and that was for the best, for it was a blackly overcast night, and whatever level of artificial illumination the city once had boasted, had long since disappeared, leaving the inhabitants to fend for themselves at night, by torchlight, campfire, or simple darkness.

Finally Buck pushed his way through the shrubbery of an ancient, overgrown archway. He patted his flight-suit, now growing dirty and tattered from his excursion through the ruined city, and pulled an old lighter from one flap-sealed pocket. He flicked it, and despite its age it lit, having been hermetically sealed and perfectly preserved during its five-hundred-year tumble through space in its owner's pocket.

Buck held the lighter before him, illuminating the base of an ancient statue, broken off centuries before at the ankles and serving now as merely a trellis for some rank and noisome ivy.

RICHARD DALEY, the pedestal of the ancient statue had carved upon it, *1902-1976*. Buck nodded in recollection of the man who had ruled the city in Buck's own boyhood days, over five hundred years ago. *The little mayor everybody liked.* There was some question about that, Buck recalled. Not everyone would have agreed to the final line.

He scrambled around through the undergrowth near the pedestal. After a while he found what he was looking for, completely hidden beneath a thick growth of ivy and hardy bushes. It was the statue of Mayor Daley, missing its feet. Of course, Buck nodded to himself, they were still up on the pedestal. Somebody had smashed in the face of the statue, Buck noted. Apparently, someone who disagreed with the line about everybody liking the old mayor.

Buck nodded and muttered something to himself. He snapped off the flame of his lighter and restored it to his pocket, then set off again at a run, Twiki following him faithfully, Theopolis bouncing from his harness around the neck of the little quad.

The pace of Buck's progress and the darkness of the city made it hard for the drone and the computer-brain to follow him. At one point they lost Buck completely, then, as Twiki stood, rotating his body and his optical sensors in hope of picking up the man again, Theopolis exclaimed, "There he is! That way, Twiki! Don't let us get lost again!"

Twiki squeaked and looked around once again. He and Theopolis could see sinister forms gathering behind them in the gloom, most of them huddling in doorways, clinging close to the walls of ruined buildings at the edges of the street, a few of the bolder ones standing in a group in the middle of the street, their number growing with every passing second as the drone and the computer seemed almost visibly to tremble with fear.

Twiki squealed frantically and Theopolis replied, his usually soothing voice somewhat higher and less steady than before. "I know, Twiki," Theopolis said. "I see them, too! Let's just keep going on after Buck. He knows what he's doing. He's our leader, and I'm sure he has a very good plan to get us out of this scrape."

Again the drone squealed in fright.

"Don't think thoughts like that," Theopolis scolded. "It runs down your batteries. There, now don't get panicky, I'm sure we can find Buck. Look, I'm sure he just went around that corner. Let's follow him."

The drone brought up short before a rusting iron fence broken by a pair of massive stone pillars and a scroll-like gate that hung from hinges broken centuries before and rusted shut. Twiki and Theopolis read the ornate scroll-like lettering that surmounted the gateway.

"Oh, my goodness. Oh, my merciful heavens, this is simply too much, simply too much for my circuits. I think I'm going to blow a fuse if this goes on."

The quad squeaked again.

"Of course I'll tell you what it says," Theopolis

placated the frantic drone. "I do wish they'd build literacy circuits into you quads, it's such a nuisance having to read to you all the time."

Squeak!

"Oh, I know it isn't your fault, Twiki. You're an absolutely splendid quad and I wouldn't trade you for any other, no matter how new and shiny he was, and no matter how many special circuits he had built into his control unit."

Squeal!

"Oh, you still want to know what it says up there, do you? I was rather hoping that you'd forgot about that, Twiki my friend. Well, I guess there's nothing for it but to tell the truth. It says, *Cemetery*."

Twiki rotated his optical sensors and squealed in terror. A group of the horrifying mutated forms was growing larger and larger behind them. Some of the more daring of the mutants were feinting moves toward the drone and his computer-friend.

"Come on, Twiki," Theopolis urged. "I know you're scared of graveyards, but we have a lot more to be frightened of from the living than we have from the dead!"

The drone scuttered forward on his short metallic legs, scuttling over the threshold of the cemetery and into the frightening, centuries-haunted domain of the departed. Here the rank growth of sickly plant-life that filled so much of Anarchia had gone completely wild. The ancient hemlocks and oleanders that stood throughout the necropolis had grown to enormous height and thickness, so that even by daylight the cemetary existed in a kind of perpetual gloom.

And now it was night, the sky was overcast, and the heavy vegetation made for a stygian blackness. Rank grasses had grown up, so the drone had to struggle constantly, not merely to make progress through the stifling growth, but even to raise his optical sensing devices above the level of the grasses.

Ancient tombstones that had not fallen completely to the ground with the passing of years, stood crazily angled, ready to catch on the footpad of any unwary passing quad. Old graves had fallen in, leaving the ground surface uneven beneath the tall, rank grasses. Because of this, Twiki quickly learned, any step might plunge him into an old grave, taking Dr. Theopolis helplessly with him.

Mausoleums, constructed to stand until Gabriel sounded the Last Trumpet on the Day of Judgment had yielded to the ravages of time. Some had been smashed flat by the terrible blast of the holocaust that created Anarchia. Others had fallen prey to the plunderers and looters who came in the wake of the blast, and still others had simply fallen in, collapsing in response to the slowly eroding forces of nature, the freezes of winter, the snows and ice of the cold season, the thaws and rains of spring, the hot baking suns of summer and the new, contracting coolness of each of five hundred autumns.

Panic-stricken, Twiki plunged from gravestone to mausoleum, squealing with each tumble that he took, scuttling away from each little echo of sound, almost shrieking with fright at the sounds of the mutant band beating the grasses in search of himself and Theopolis and the complex circuits and rare, precious metals that they hoped to salvage from the two machines.

Suddenly Twiki's metal foot caught on the hidden edge of a fallen gravestone and he found himself tumbling not onto the grassy turf of the cemetery, but the prostrate, grieving form of Buck Rogers.

Twiki squeaked.

Dr. Theopolis, his lights blinking and glowing in a virtual kaleidoscope of forms and colors, exclaimed, "Buck! We've found you!"

The only light was the eerie shifting array of colors provided by the facelike display pattern on Dr. Theopolis's control panel. Even in this pale and shifting illumination the two machine-people could see that Buck's back was heaving, not with injury or exertion, but with the strength of the emotion that he felt.

Twiki managed to right himself, and as he did so the lights of Dr. Theopolis's facelike panel illuminated the gravestone upon which Buck had flung himself.

In the pale, eerie light, Theopolis scanned the inscription. Twiki squealed his impatience and the computer-brain read aloud the words carved upon the marble:

EDNA AND JAMES ROGERS
THEIR SON FRANK AND
DAUGHTER MARILYN
APRIL

There was no date or year. If they had ever been inscribed on the marble headstone, they had long ago been lost to the ravages of some violent act.

As Twiki and Theopolis stood silently, Buck Rogers slowly rose from the stone. He held his lighter in his hand—obviously, he had used it to read the headstone before Twiki arrived with Dr. Theopolis to give illumination. There were tears in Buck Rogers's eyes. He recognized the two metallic beings and nodded to them in acknowledgement of their presence.

"At least I know part of it," Buck said. "My parents, my brother and sister . . . of course there were others. What's happened to them is still unknown."

He breathed deeply, getting better control of himself. "Of course, if all of that was five hundred years ago, I don't suppose it really matters any more. Did they know what had happened to me, before they died? Did they live on for five more years—or fifty? Well," he shrugged, "at least I've seen their grave. For whatever that may be worth."

"Buck," Theopolis said soothingly. "I don't mean to intrude on your hour of grief."

Buck gazed down at the computer-brain hanging from the neck of the drone.

"But we can't really stay here," Theopolis resumed. "We, ah—somebody followed us here. Twiki and me. It would be very dangerous for us to stay here. Ah, maybe even fatal, Buck."

Buck was still caught up in his grief. It was as if he were divorced from the reality of the moment and had been thrown back through time to unravel the mystery of the fate of his family and friends.

"What happened to them?" he asked. "There's no date on the marker. And there's only one marker for Mother and Dad and Marilyn and Frank. What could have happened to them? And to the others?"

"Only the few fortunate ones were buried at all," Theopolis supplied. "It happened to them so fast, Buck. Families were buried together. Dates became unimportant when all the systems of civilization broke down.

"There were no newspapers or television any more. People lost track. Living was strictly day-to-day. At first it was thought that the first few millions who died in the holocaust were the end of the horror. But the war went on, and more died. More war, more killing, more war, more killing.

"Finally the fighting stopped only because there were no more armies left to fight. There were only the tattered survivors, struggling to survive in the face of starvation, contamination, radiation, and then—plague."

Buck knelt once again and pressed his forehead to the cold stone. "God bless them," he whispered. "I'd go back there and die at their side if I had my way."

"But you can't, Buck. The past is gone." All of the agitation, all of the past hours' part-serious, part-mocking terror and banter was gone from Theopolis's voice. He was as serious now as ever he had been, and Buck understood the real concern that he heard in Theopolis's statement.

For the first time he had a full understanding of a strange fact concerning the computer-brain.

Back in Buck's own time there had been long and heated debate as to whether computers could really think and/or feel. Engineers and programmers at the great university computing laboratories and at the research centers of the huge electronics companies had been able to build and program machines that could convincingly simulate both emotion and intelligence.

But—were these merely simulations, or were the machines really thinking? Were they really feeling? What *was* thought? What *was* emotion?

One early and clever experiment had involved placing a series of volunteer subjects on one end of a telephone line, the other end of which might be connected to a trained conversational specialist . . . or to a computer. Sometimes it was one, sometimes the other.

The volunteers were permitted to converse over the telephone for as long as they wished, until they were convinced that they knew the identity of the voice on the other end of the line. They were then instructed to terminate the conversation and mark on a score card whether they believed they had been speaking with a human being or with a cleverly programmed machine.

After a series of dry runs that were used to refine the computer program, the sponsors of the experiment began keeping records of the volunteers' judgments. They discovered that the rate of correct identifications was equally high, whether the second conversationalist was a person or a machine.

But that didn't convince anyone!

Those who had believed, before the experiment, that machines could really think and feel, claimed that their position had been vindicated.

And those who believed that machines could only mimic the outward evidence of thought or feeling, wound up as convinced as ever, that *their* own position had been vindicated!

As an astronaut, Buck was expected to become thoroughly familiar with the programming and performance and even, to a certain extent, the circuitry of advanced computing machinery. He had wound up a skeptic on the big question—not quite fully convinced, but heavily inclined to think that computers only simulated human thought and feeling.

But now, with Dr. Theopolis offering his solace and his counsel in the hour of Buck's grief, the astronaut felt himself convinced at last that the computer-brain was not merely simulating human characteristics. Buck decided that Theopolis was truly thinking and truly feeling the emotions that he expressed.

And in that moment it became clear to Buck for the first time that his whole strange experience was also real. The twentieth century and all its people were dead and gone. This bizarre new world of the twenty-fifth century with its quads and computer-brains, its magnificent domed Inner Cities and its seething, rubble-filled Anarchias, its Defense Squadron and space pirates and Draconian Empire, were all very, very real. And if he intended to live, he would have to close his mind to the world of his boyhood and learn to live in this brave new world, faulted and imperfect though it was!

He started to express his thanks to Dr. Theopolis but he was interrupted by the frantic squealing of Twiki. Startled, Buck peered into the gloom beyond the drone. A chorus of grunts and inchoate shouts were echoing from the far corners of the graveyard.

"You can't save your past," Dr. Theopolis murmured softly to Buck, "but you can help us survive in the present and in the future, Buck . . . if there *is* any future!"

Even in the murkiness of the cemetery, Buck was able to see that a virtual wall of the horrifying mutants was moving slowly but relentlessly forward, threatening at moments to break into a final, fatal attack upon himself and Theopolis and Twiki.

"Get behind me, quick!" Buck snapped at the quad. With Theopolis firmly hung about his neck, Twiki scuttled behind the astronaut.

Buck knelt for a moment, not in renewed meditation or final, this-is-the-hour-of-our-death type of prayer, but in order to snatch up a handful of the tall, dry, parched weeds that grew rankly throughout the cemetery. With one hand he held the weeds before him; with the other, he flicked his lighter into life, its tiny butane flame flaring luridly against the murk.

The weeds smouldered for a second. They were dry but not entirely dry. The night was far advanced, dew had already settled throughout the burying ground, and the dry weeds had been redampened by atmospheric condensation. Acrid smoke rose from the weeds. Buck didn't know how much more fuel his lighter held, nor how much longer the mutants would delay their charge. At the moment they seemed to have been halted more by curiosity than by any other motive.

With a low growl the apparent leader of the mutant band signed that he had had enough of this strange show. It was time to launch the final attack!

The mutants sprang just at the moment that the weeds glowed for a moment, than sprang into bright, flaring flame!

The leading mutant tumbled forward, landed almost in Buck's arms. His face and hands smashed into Buck as the horrifying creature screamed with pain and terror as his flesh was bathed in the searing flames. He leaped backwards, ran screaming across the uneven earth of the burying ground.

Some of the other mutants followed in his wake, but the remainder of the raider-band merely backed away, frightened, clearly, of the flame, yet not so frightened as to give up the prospect of this little group of potential victims.

Buck took a step forward, gathering more weeds to add to his makeshift torch. Step by step the mutants retreated before him, but so numerous were they that their band closed in again behind Buck and the others. Now, saved though they were for the briefest of moments, they found themselves trapped again, completely surrounded by the raiders!

"Quick," Buck commanded Twiki and Dr. Theopolis, "hop onto my back! No discussion, move!"

They obeyed as quickly as Buck had spoken. Grasping Dr. Theopolis firmly in one hand so he wouldn't swing loose at the jump, little Twiki squealed once and launched himself with surprising strength and accuracy, if no great amount of grace, into the air. He landed on Buck's tall shoulders, grabbed the astronaut with his free hand, settled Dr. Theopolis with the other, then clutched firmly at Buck Rogers's neck and shoulders.

"Hang on tight," Buck gritted, " 'cause here we go!"

He bent and started a row-fire from the flaming weeds in his hands, skipping along, bending and setting fires, advancing a short distance and setting some more, extending the line he had created, slowly drawing a solid wall of flame between himself and his two machine-passengers on one side, and the mutant raiders on the other.

Painfully but steadily they made their way across the graveyard in that fashion, Buck having to replenish his handheld torch every few dozen yards, while he watched the mutants dancing in impotent hatred on the other side of the row of flames that he raised. At the rusted iron gateway of the cemetery, Buck made a final flying leap, rolled onto the roadway outside, carefully dislodging Twiki as he did so. In a matter of seconds they were standing side by side, turning back for a quick glimpse of the cemetery as the enraged mutant raiders poured from its mouth, setting off in hot pursuit of their escaping prey.

"They haven't quit," Buck shouted. "Come on!"

With Twiki at his side, Theopolis riding the drone as usual, Buck set off as fast as he could sprint, down the center of the cracked pavement. Here, outside the graveyard, the night was not quite as completely murk-shrouded as it was beneath the giant trees and overgrown shrubbery within the cemetery.

Over his shoulder Buck could see the leader of

the mutant band run to an old lamp post and seize a broken metal pipe from the gutter. He hefted the iron implement and began smashing it against the metal lamp post, sending up a resounding series of almost deafening clangs. The horrid man-thing kept up the deafening clanging for a time. Then Buck could hear a similar clamor resounding from across the city.

For an instant Buck thought it was an actual echo of the pipe being wielded against the lamp post. Then he detected a difference in tone. Soon a third clamor joined the two, and another, and another, until the chill night air was filled with a deafening arhythmic cacophony that set Buck's teeth on edge and made the hairs at the back of his neck rise in shuddering sympathy.

He ran, Twiki and Theopolis at his side, for block after ancient city block, but no matter how he dodged or turned or sped across the cracked pavement, the cacophonous clanging stayed with him and Theopolis and Twiki. Finally, he stopped, his breath rasping in and out of his aching lungs in great, desperate gasps.

"What—" he tried to ask.

"What—is it?" he managed to get the question out.

Theopolis had no problem with breath, of course. "It's a rather primitive communication system amongst the mutants," he explained in a calm, professorial tone.

"The poor devils," his lights glowed sympathetically, "they stick together when they think they've found valuable prey. Rather than lose important salvage and loot, they are willing to share all with one another."

"Who're you worried about?" Buck asked, his breathing now back nearly to normal, "the mutants —or us?"

Twiki squealed and Buck glanced around.

At the nearest intersection a band of mutants were moving into the roadway to block the path that Buck and Twiki and Dr. Theopolis would normally have taken. Buck and Twiki turned around, ready to make their way out of the other end of the city block.

But this too was closed off by a band of ragged raiders!

Buck and Twiki turned back the way they had been facing. This was their original group of foes, the mutant raiders who had almost succeeded in capturing and "salvaging" them in the weed-choked cemetery. The mob had been advancing rapidly behind the backs of their intended victims; in the full sight of their faces they slowed their pace to a walk, to little more than a creep.

Still, slowly they advanced, step by step reducing the distance between themselves and the astronaut and his mechanical companions.

It was as if they were savoring the tension and the anticipation of the kill, like a sadistic hunter hovering over a trapped wolf in the Alaskan wild, eager to make his kill, yet hesitant to end the pleasure of leading up to it.

"Thanks, Buck," the astronaut heard Theopolis' voice. "Thanks for making a good try of it. You gave your best."

"It isn't over yet, Theopolis!" Buck exclaimed. "Twiki, this is going to be a one-shot. We'll make it on the first try, or we're done for."

The quad squealed.

"For once you don't have to translate, Theopolis," Buck said. "On my back again, Twiki!"

The little robot jumped, clasped Buck just as Buck ran for the sidewalk, charged across it to the nearest building and leaped into the air. His fingertips barely scraped the bottom rung of a rusted, ancient fire-escape ladder.

Buck would never know how he did it, but somehow he managed to cling to that old iron rung for the few precious seconds that he had to. As the man hung there, panting with effort, the little robot clinging to his shoulders and the computer brain wedged precariously between them, the fire-escape ladder slowly slid downward, its hinges screaming with the accumulated rust of five hundred years of weather and disuse.

As soon as the ladder was down Buck released his grip on the bottom rung, scampered up the ladder, leaped onto the first storey platform of the old tenement house and tugged with all his strength to pull the ladder back up, just as the bravest of the attacking mutants reached the ladder and reached for the iron, hoping to duplicate Buck's astonishing feat.

The mutant missed by fractions where Buck had succeeded by a similarly narrow margin.

Frustrated again as they had been by Buck's clever maneuver in the cemetery, the mutants and their newly arrived allies set up a dancing and a keening wail of fury and grief.

"What can we do now?" Theopolis quavered. "You've saved us twice, Buck, but each time only temporarily. I don't want you to think I'm unappreciative of your efforts, but aren't we still as good as doomed? If they can't get this ladder down and climb up after us, and if they can't just wait to starve us out . . . won't they somehow make their way through this old building and come at us through the windows?"

"I don't know," Buck conceded.

"Then we're finished," the computer mourned.

"I didn't say that," Buck disagreed. "I don't know the solution yet, but we can work on one! And I'll tell you one thing, you old box of transistors."

"What's that?" Theopolis asked.

"If we have to sit tight and figure out a solution, I'd sure as hell rather sit up here and do it," Buck pointed at the fire escape where they huddled, "than be down there in the middle of that mob trying to find a way to escape!"

"You're right, of course," Theopolis said. "I've got to learn that you never give up, Captain Rogers, and that as long as you keep searching for a solution, there's always a chance that you may just find one!"

Buck grunted and tried to concentrate on the situation, but the dancing, screeching mob beneath them suddenly changed its behavior. From a great distance Buck could hear a clanging again, the sound of iron pipes being pounded on derelict lamp posts, but there was a subtle difference to the rhythm and the pattern of the strokes. It was like the famous jungle telegraph of Africa back in the days of the nineteenth century. Long before Europeans arrived and set up their so-called modern communications systems, the old civilizations had evolved their own methods of sending messages for hundreds or even thousands of miles by setting up series of repeater-stations of drummers, like the booster circuits on long-distance telephone lines.

And these mutants, pitiful, half-human wretches though they were, had reinvented the jungle telegraph, sending messages from end to end of the great wrecked city of Anarchia by pounding out different rhythms with iron pipes on rusting, ancient lamp posts!

Buck looked down into the street where the mutant mob had gathered, and saw its members scampering off in all directions, obviously bent on some mission far more urgent than trying to coax one ancient astronaut and two modern mechanical creatures down from the rusted fire escape of a ruined building!

Suddenly Twiki showed that he understood the situation's newest twist, even more rapidly than either Buck Rogers or Dr. Theopolis had. The little drone began to leap up and down on the rusted platform, squeaking joyously and hugging Buck with both metallic arms.

Theopolis's lights burst into an astonishing semblance of a grand happy grin. "I agree with Twiki," he said in his again-mellow voice. "Very good, Buck. Bravo, bravo! How in the world did you manage that?"

"Manage what?" Buck asked in puzzlement.

Before the computer could answer the air was split by the sound of a siren, a new and utterly unique sound here in the ruined city of Anarchia. Realization dawned in Buck's brain. "Oh, ho!" he said. "I see! We can give credit for the sudden dispersement of the mutants to whoever is sounding that siren."

"That's right," Theopolis added. "I've never heard of such a thing, Buck. They surely wouldn't do that for a couple of machines, eh, Twiki? You must be one important fellow, Captain, for the Inner City to react as they have."

"But how *have* they reacted?" Buck demanded. "I'm new in town, remember? What does that siren mean?"

"It means they've sent a force into Anarchia,"

Theopolis said. "That siren is the Inner City force approaching, and they just don't do that. As far as Inner City is concern, Anarchia is quarantined. They exile their criminals here, but they never let them back in, and nobody from Inner City *ever* comes here voluntarily!"

Twiki began to jump up and down, squealing shrilly with excitement. Buck and Theopolis both stared down into the now-deserted thoroughfare. The bulk of the fleeing mutants had all left by one end of the street, and from the other there now came first the sound, then the sight of a heavily armored vehicle, equipped with weapons as well as shielding against both radiation and missile attack.

Six armed troopers leaped from the vehicle and set up an immediate defense perimeter around its metallic bulk. A seventh uniformed officer climbed from the vehicle, studied the situation and advanced to take command of the party. One of the six heavily armed troopers addressed the commanding officer.

"Colonel!"

The single word was used to attract the commander's attention. The trooper pointed up toward the fire-escape balcony where Buck still watched along with Theopolis and Twiki.

The commander followed the trooper's pointed finger. From the escape balcony Buck could make out clearly the face of the military leader.

It was Colonel Wilma Deering of the Intercept Squadron!

"Good evening, Captain," Wilma called up from the street. "I wonder if I could interest you in a proposition."

Buck smiled down from the balcony with gratitude and a sense of admiration that bordered on something far warmer and more personal. Without saying a word, he and Theopolis and Twiki started to climb down from the fire escape.

SIX

~~~~~~

The squadron of Starfighters streaked away from their launching pads and lanced into the deep blue heavens above the Inner City. At the astonishing power and rate-of-climb ratings of these ultramodern combat craft, they quickly rose above the earth's atmosphere and the blue refracted sunlight was replaced by the black of cislunar space, a velvety black sprinkled with glittering stars like shimmering diamond chips even in bright daylight hours.

Each Starfighter was a sleek object that might well have stood, in classical times, as a work of some genius sculptor. Their curves were graceful yet strong, their skins showed a smooth sheen that could have been designed as much for its ability to please the observer's eye as it was to protect their internal components and their pilots from the radiation of space, the heat of atmospheric resistance on launching and reentry, or the impact of enemy lasers or missile blasts.

The entire Intercept Squadron had left its launching pads. This was no combat mission—it was a routine training and shakedown cruise for all the pilots save one, but even the most veteran of Starfighter pilots was expected to fly regular training missions in order to stay at the razor's edge of keen skill and combat readiness.

If ever Earth faced invasion from the starlanes, the Intercept Squadron was not only her first line of defense, but in a sense her last as well. For an alien starship force, smashing down the barriers of Earth's extended defense line, would be free to blast away at surface installations until the planet lay prostrate and helpless before the hobnailed boots of an army of invasion and occupation.

It was up to the Intercept Squadron to prevent that from ever happening.

And today a new pilot was training with the squadron. He was by far the oldest aviator ever to take a ship up from the surface of the planet Earth. He was more than five hundred years old: Captain Buck Rogers.

Inside Buck's sleek Starfighter the intercom hummed softly with a carrier wave, and the voice of the squadron commander, Colonel Wilma Deering, spoke into Buck's ear. "Stay close on my wing, Captain. We'll keep the maneuvers nice and simple." This was not the warm, feminine Wilma Deering whom Buck had crushed in his arms for one swift embrace in the middle of Anarchia's rubble-strewn street. This was Colonel Deering, all military prowess and cold efficiency.

"Stay on AutoFlight," Colonel Deering continued. "You won't be expected to run anything but the throttle on this mission."

Buck felt a rush of hot, angry blood to his cheeks. He had been a top Air Force fighter-jockey in the earliest years of his aerial career. Then, with the advent of the last, uneasy peace that preceded the final holocaust he had become a crack test pilot and astronaut.

And now this wisecracking, overconfident woman, this hotshot colonel who hadn't been born when he was a fully rated space exploration pilot, was telling *him* not to touch anything on his own ship except for the throttle! "Thanks a lot, colonel," he gritted resentfully, "is it all right if I look out the window once in a while, or am I supposd to sit here and study the operator's manual while I fly?"

"This is no time for levity!" Wilma snapped back. Her eyes showed an angry annoyance at the new pilot's insubordinate attitude.

"We've lost nearly a third of our ships in this vector to pirates," she told him. "When they hit, they hit fast. You can't outfly a computer. Your reflexes just aren't as fast as its are. So let the ship take care of any necessary evasive action to avoid

those training missiles. If you get in the way of
one you'll cost us an expensive ship, as well as
the trouble of training a replacement for yourself.
And the Inner City tax rates are high enough
now!"

"I appreciate your concern," Buck told her. "I
just wish I'd brought along a copy of *Thrilling
Wonder Stories* to read."

Wilma Deering started to respond, then halted.
Her eyes snapped wide. She opened a channel to
the entire squadron. "Commanding officer here. I
make a target on vector four zero one."

Another pilot responded. "Roger, Colonel. I have
visual on a target just to starboard."

"Check range," Wilma instructed the pilot. "If
you have visual at this apparent distance, it must
be gigantic!"

Through the window of his own sleek Starfighter, Buck Rogers had sighted in on the flying
behemoth. "You've never seen anything like this,
lady, I'll bet on that! Not even in the twenty-fifth
century!"

From the Draconian flagship, long-range space-
telescopes kept the terran Intercept Squadron
carefully in view from the moment its gleaming,
needle-nosed ships poked their snouts above
Earth's seething atmosphere to the instant they
arrived in deep space and commenced to swarm
around the Draconian behemoth like a horde of

frantic bumblebees swooping and dancing in the air around a grizzly.

The Princess Ardala had received word of the first sighting of the Intercept Squadron's blastoff. From that moment onward, at her stern command, she was kept informed by the lookout bridge of every move, every significant maneuver, of the tiny, swarming, streamlined interceptors.

Kane had assumed personal command of the lookout bridge, and maintained constant electronic contact with the princess, but now he turned over command of the bridge to a Draconian subordinate of unquestioned competence and loyalty, and trotted anxiously through the corridors and companionways of the ship to the princess's personal stateroom in order to apprise her, face-to-face, of the startling message received on the bridge from the earth ships.

When she heard the request, Princess Ardala's face assumed an expression of astonishment.

"Permission to come aboard," she repeated the Earth ships' request. "But why, Kane?"

"They claim they're escorting a special envoy, Ardala. And that's all they'll say."

"But that isn't according to protocol!" The princess paced uneasily, the lines of a puzzled frown marring her normally flawless physiognomy.

"I don't like this, Kane," she grumbled petulantly. "I don't like this even one little bit. What could they possibly be up to?"

"I don't know," Kane replied. "But if we refuse them permission to come aboard we'll rouse their suspicions."

"And if we let them come aboard, Kane, then we'll *confirm* their suspicions. We're in a gorgeous double-bind, an absolutely gorgeous double-bind."

She stopped pacing and glared at him, the superior conferring with a subordinate. "I want your recommendation, Kane. You're always patting yourself on the back and claiming you're such a grand strategist. Let's hear a plan from you!"

"Of course, my princess, of course." Kane's previously gruff manner was replaced by an oily confidence, as if Ardala's demand for a plan from him was exactly what he'd been maneuvering for. "We're not in a double-bind at all, Ardala. We've had plenty of warning. As soon as the bridge sighted the Earth interceptors I ordered preparations aboard the ship. They can come aboard and wander around to their hearts' delight, and they'll find nothing whatever to make them suspicious."

Ardala smiled in relief. "Well, that changes things, Kane. You *do* have a brain after all. Issue commands for the communications bridge to message the earth squadron that they'll be most cordially welcomed aboard. Have the flight deck prepare to receive the landing party." She laughed a low, sinister laugh that raised the hairs on the back of even Kane's bull-neck. "And send word that I will personally receive the special envoy who's coming up to see us."

The princess disappeared behind a dressing screen and continued her conversation with the oily mannered Kane. When she reappeared from behind the screen she had exchanged her satiny lounging costume for a more elaborate but highly provocative court outfit. "Do I look fit to receive Earth's special envoy?" the princess asked Kane.

He nodded and grunted his approval, not trusting himself to utter a word to the splendidly voluptuous princess.

With Tigerman, Ardala's fierce, huge bodyguard, hovering behind her, the princess and Kane advanced across the great ship's flight deck to greet the newcomers. Colonel Wilma Deering and Captain Buck Rogers led the Earth party, followed by three other veteran pilots.

Kane spoke the first ceremonial words:

"Welcome aboard the flagship *Draconia,* representing the Emperor Draco, Conqueror of Space, Warlord of Astrium, and Supreme Ruler of the Draconian Realm. I present to you the Princess Ardala, daughter of our king."

The princess greeted the Earth party graciously. "I am most delighted to receive you. This pleasure is an unexpected one. We were hardly prepared to greet you with proper circumstance."

"Your presence alone, your highness, is far more than adequate greeting," Wilma Deering replied with like ceremony. "I am Colonel Deering, Commander of the Third Force of the Earth Directorate. With me are my senior officers. And I believe you have already met Captain Rogers."

Buck stepped forward, a grin on his face. He bowed slightly, reached for the princess's hand and planted a kiss on it.

"A most promising foretaste of what to expect on Earth, I'm sure." She looked straight into Wilma's eyes. "But no, I'm sure that if I'd ever met so dashing a young captain, it would not be an event I would easily forget."

Buck shot a quick glance at the princess, found her gazing at him. "I can't say that I've had the pleasure," she remarked.

Buck received a wilting glance from Wilma, ignored it, turned a charming smile on the princess. "I think you're mistaken, princess," Buck muttered, "I never forget a knuckle."

"Captain," Wilma interrupted.

Buck became more businesslike. "Listen, we came a long way to get to the bottom of things. Would you like me to describe some of the inner sections of this ship, to prove I've been here before?"

"Please, Captain Rogers. Stop."

Ardala's curiosity was aroused. "What inner sections?"

"Just the sections of his mind," Wilma replied drily.

"Aw, now, that's hitting above the belt," Buck complained. "I may not be memorable to the princess, but I'll never forget her. I especially love that dress with the peacock feathers. They set off your neck so beautifully!"

Wilma turned to another officer. "Major, please guide Captain Rogers and the rest of our pilots to their ships."

"But we haven't told the princess why we came, yet," Buck complained. "The pirate forces are at their worst in this sector. We brought our ships up to escort the princess's ship and assure its safe arrival."

"That's very reassuring, Captain," Kane commented smoothly.

Wilma attempted again to shut off the conversation. "Captain Rogers!" she repeated.

"As a matter of fact," Buck went on, "if you would like us to attach a squadron directly on board your ship . . . just to be on hand in case of attack, you see. . . ."

"Most generous of you," Kane said. "Most generous, Captain . . . Colonel Deering. But I'm sure that your mere presence in this vector will assure our security."

"And it is the strict interpretation of our mutual treaty," Princess Ardala added, "that this ship not bear arms of any kind. I would interpret that to mean . . . arms . . . from either side."

"I had a feeling you'd interpret it that way," Buck commented.

From Wilma Deering's point of view the conversation had been an unmitigated disaster, starting with Buck's kissing that horrible space vamp's hand and ending with the quarrel over the neutrality treaty. The best she could do was to end it as fast as possible. "To your gracious majesty," she said, "our thanks and our prayers for a safe arrival. I wish you good day."

"Good day," Ardala replied, smiling smugly. She started to turn away.

Suddenly—a resounding shock rocked the ship.

"What in Draco's name!" Ardala exclaimed.

Kane reacted instantly, shoving Tigerman forward to guard the princess. "Protect her! Attention! Alert all stations! Secure ship!"

A voice echoed through the deck, coming from the bridge above. "Hostile aircraft approaching. Ship under attack!"

"So this is how you bid us safe conduct," Kane snarled at Wilma. "Well, at least you and your fellow traitors will die with us!"

Wilma Deering ignored the insulting accusation, turning instead toward her own party. "To your ships—now!"

Along with the others, Buck forgot all about the just-ended confrontation and put his attention into the emergency. He scanned the deck, looking for the source of the explosions. He took a final quick glance at Kane before running for his interceptor ship, and found himself met with a glare of unspoken hatred.

"Okay, pal," Buck shot out, "we'll meet again!"

The pilots scampered to reach their ships. Just

as Buck jumped for the entry hatch of his, he saw Wilma standing and glaring at him. "You are under arrest, Captain," the colonel snapped.

"Sure," Buck answered. "You gonna put handcuffs on me now, or can I use both hands to fly this toy?"

"You are disqualified for all combat operations, Captain Rogers! You will return directly to Earth and land there, under arrest!"

But Buck didn't hear the words. He was already inside his ship, busily dogging the hatch and the pilot's canopy.

Meanwhile the sky around the Draconian flagship was filled with swarming, gaudily painted pirate ships. A marauder decorated with extravagant dragons' heads screamed across the sky, making a pass at the *Draconia*. The raider sent a cluster of fireballs blasting at the flagship.

The *Draconia*'s early warning net had functioned in time, and the Earth interceptors made their escape from the great ship, swarming away from its monstrous bulk to counterattack the dancing, lethal pirate craft. Buck Rogers, handling his interceptor with an ease and familiarity learned in hundreds of mission-hours half a millenium before, shoved the Starfighter through a sudden snap-roll, righted the ship, found a pirate craft angling in at him from an insanely high angle.

Buck wheeled away, saw the marauder flash by over his shoulder. The one major difference between combat in space and in the air was that aircraft, even though operating in three dimensions, had a constant reference point of the Earth. Up and down were relative concepts, but always relative to the planet's surface. Here in deep space the same three dimensions obtained, but there was no up, no down. He was fighting within a completely free-form medium.

A second marauder craft streaked in, following the lead of the first. Buck was in the clear, at least momentarily, but the second marauder swerved to attack another Starfighter. "Heads up, major!" Buck shouted. "Enemy craft on your tail. Hit a roll, I'll pick him up!"

The second Starfighter rolled, turned, snapping through the maneuvers that were programmed into its ship's computers. The enemy craft stayed dangerously close behind, matching the Starfighter's maneuvers move for move.

"Not that way," Buck radio'd, "you're rolling right into his power!"

The marauder craft fired its lasers, the Starfighter tried to move out of the path of the deadly weapons but the marauder craft seemed to anticipate its every move. There was a horrendous blooming of flame and flying, white-hot fragments as the Starfighter, caught fully by the laser blast, exploded through space.

Buck clutched the controls of his Starfighter, his fine-tuned instincts guiding the spacecraft through its maneuvers while his mind recoiled in horror from the sight he had just beheld.

Nearby in her own craft, Wilma Deering shared similar emotions. She scanned the blackness around her, picking out the maneuvering marauders and Starfighters. Spotting Buck's Starfighter she switched on her radio and snapped a command to the captain. "Rogers—I ordered you back to Earth!"

"Colonel Deering, you need all the help you can get," Buck replied. Before he could say anything more he spotted another Starfighter in dire peril. "Look out, Baker," Buck cried. "He's on you!"

The young pilot Buck had warned swung around in panic. He spotted a marauder on his tail, about to fire its deadly lasers at his Starfighter.

"Pull up," Buck shouted, "I can cut him off!"

Baker pushed the automatic evasion button in his cockpit. It was the same button that had led the major to his destruction minutes earlier. The Starfighter rolled away, the marauder craft holding course with it, move for move, turn for turn. After two quick rolls, the marauder fired its lasers.

Baker's Starfighter blossomed into a second of the deadly fireballs, flames rolling away from the destroyed fuselage, white-hot fragments flying in all directions.

"You jackass!" Buck despaired.

Wilma choked back a cry of horror as she saw Baker's ship blossom into flame. Suddenly she found the sky on fire around her own Starfighter.

She whirled frantically in her pilot's seat, saw a marauder streaking after her. Desperately she pressed the red flashing evade button.

Her Starfighter went into its automatically programmed maneuvers, rolling across the sky. The marauder craft followed, matching move for move.

Buck watched in shock, flicked on his radio, shouted at Wilma, "Take it down, Colonel! Straight down! Don't roll! Throw on your space-flaps!"

"I can't!" Wilma cried in response. "It's against all the principles of modern space combat!"

And the sky began to explode all around her.

Buck shook his head, muttering half to himself, "Where'd you guys learn to fly! You'd never have made it past basic aero in my day, no less got certied for space combat." Buck pushed a button on his control board. A yellow light flashed on the indicator panel. Etched lettering on it read, *Manual override*. Buck reached for a control lever, took a firm hold on it and swung it hard over.

He brought his craft in behind another Starfighter under heavy marauder attack. The marauder as usual was able to match its course perfectly with the Starfighter's. As the heavy attacker came within laser range it seemed inevitable that still another Starfighter was shortly to blossom into flame and flying fragments.

Instead, Buck's ship flashed across the sky, streaking to a point above and beside the maneuvering pair. Buck dived, swung through a difficult

Immelmann, streaked toward the marauder from nine o'clock and pressed his firing stud once, twice.

This time it was the marauder rather than the Starfighter that blossomed into flame. For once Buck was able to grin . . . as was the pilot of the rescued Starfighter, Colonel Wilma Deering!

Buck pulled his Starfighter alongside Wilma's, tossed her an old-fashioned thumbs-up salute and a grin, then streaked away, leaving the colonel to reexamine her notions of military doctrine—and her feelings about Captain William "Buck" Rogers!

While aboard the *Draconia*, Princess Ardala stood watching the aerial combat ending in the vacuum above her observation bridge. The marauder craft streaked away, abandoning their attack on the flagship, leaving the surviving Starfighters to circle triumphantly over the broad decks of the *Draconia*.

Princess Ardala spoke aloud, knowing that radio pickups would capture her voice and carry it to Wilma Deering and the rest of her Intercept Squadron. "The people of Draconia thank you for your brave support, Colonel," Ardala intoned, "and also bereave your losses. May our Father's light guide you to safety. And may our impending arrival on your planet be equally blessed. Please inform your Council that the peace mission is arriving and ask them to proceed with the appropriate ceremonies."

Back in space, Wilma watched Buck's ship streak away. She switched on her radio and said,

"Now, Captain—let's go home." She watched Buck's ship and the few other survivors drop away from the flagship *Draconia* and into their reentry orbits. Then she threw her own Starfighter into a wingover and dropped back toward earth.

At the Intercept Squadron hangar, Buck Rogers walked deliberately away from his ship. Wilma had landed shortly behind him and ran from her own Starfighter to catch up with Buck. "Captain Rogers," she called. Buck halted, waited for her to speak. "I know you expect undying gratitude for what you did up there," Wilma said, "and I suppose you did save my life."

"I was saving a Starfighter," Buck answered bitterly. "You told me there was a short supply of them, and I can see why now."

"Your approval of our flying skills is inconsequential," Wilma Deering snapped. "You won't be flying with us again!"

"None of you'll be flying for long, if you don't get rid of whoever's programming your defense tactics!"

"*I* designed our tactics, Captain Rogers. They have seen us through a nearly endless war and have kept us in command of the skies throughout its duration."

"Didn't look that great to me up there," Buck said sardonically.

Wilma conceded, "We have suffered casualties unusually high since encountering those pirates. I don't know why. . . ."

"I do," Buck bounded back. "They know every move you're going to make before you make it!"

"That's impossible!"

"I saw it, Colonel. Take my word for it, if I hadn't shut off my flight computer and gone onto manual, neither you nor I would be here now. You've got a spy, all right, but it isn't me." He turned away and again started to walk toward the headquarters shack.

"Wait," Wilma cried. "Captain Rogers, the princess denied your story. I have no choice but to arrest you, pending a renewed proceeding in your case." He kept on walking. "Captain Rogers! Don't make me shoot you again!"

Buck turned back and saw Wilma's hand resting on the holster that held her laser pistol. "Wilma," Buck said, "where can I go? The only home that I know isn't just miles away, it's separated from us by centuries! There's no place for me to hide. So just forget this silly arrest stuff, and get your act together."

As he had before, Buck simply turned his back and walked away. But this time he heard no count, nor did Wilma unholster her laser. Instead she stood confused, watching Buck Rogers's form diminish as he crossed the landing pad. She muttered under her breath, whispering angry curses that would have curled the hair of a longshoreman in Buck Rogers's time, yet fighting to keep the tears in her eyes from spilling over onto her softly rounded cheeks. Her mood held for a few seconds, then was broken by a mellow, soothing voice.

"Colonel Deering, have you seen Captain Rogers?" It was none other than Dr. Theopolis, his plastic case cleaned and polished to show no sign of his ordeal in Anarchia. He hung from the neck of his drone Twiki, also cleaned up, refurbished, and restored to perfect condition.

"That man Rogers is a primitive barbarian," Wilma grumbled.

Theopolis said simply, "Oh?"

"Not to mention," Wilma continued, "a liar!"

"Oh, dear," Theopolis said, "I *am* sorry to hear that. It's going to make matters very, very awkward that you feel that way."

"Sending Captain Rogers back to Anarchia will not be awkward. And this time there will be no rescue expedition!"

"But I'm afraid . . . that there is." Theopolis paused, his lights flashing in confused patterns. "You see, Wilma my dear, our Council has had a formal request from her majesty, the Princess Ardala."

"What's that got to do with Buck Rogers?" Wilma demanded.

"Everything," Theopolis said. "They wish to decorate him for valor. With the Draconian Order of Merit or some such award. The *princess* says that he single-handedly saved her unarmed flagship from attack by the renegade pirates."

"Did you say *single-handedly?*"

"Apparently, even your command ship was nearly destroyed, Wilma. Were it not for Captain Rogers's inordinate skills and quick thinking, the princess feels that—"

"I'm not interested in what the princess feels," Wilma cut him off agitatedly. "I know what happened. I was there."

She turned away and began to cross the field, anger and resentment visible in every line of her trim body. "And what's more," she called back at Theopolis, "if Captain Rogers is to remain out of custody, then I am personally going to see that you are held responsible for him. Wherever he goes, whatever he does! And whatever the consequences! Good day, Doctor!"

She disappeared, and now it was Theopolis's turn to grumble in distress. "Dear me, dear me, did you hear that, Twiki? If the captain does anything wrong, we're all going to end up back in Anarchia again!"

Twiki stood still for a moment, for all the world as if he was concentrating on Theopolis's prediction. Then he began to scuttle across the landing pad, zigging and zagging like a broken-field runner. "Twiki," Theopolis cried, "stop this! Where do you think we're going? This is no time to get hysterical. Twiki, please, come to your senses at once!"

Wilma Deering by now had reached the office of her friend and mentor, the aged scientist Dr. Huer. She entered to find him with his back to the entryway, his hands clasped in the small of his waist, gazing abstractly from the window. Before him stretched the magnificent vista of the Inner City, its gleaming spires reaching nearly to touch the inner surface of the great arching dome that held the city in, held the poisoned air and vicious denizens of Anarchia without.

Huer turned as Wilma entered and listened patiently as she poured out her concern over the situation with the pirates, the dogfight, and her distressing relationship with Captain Buck Rogers. When she finished, Huer said, "I'm inclined to think that the pirates and Buck are the least of our worries. The Council was too quick to accept this treaty with the Draconians. They took them at face value, and I fear that was a mistake."

"It was understandable," Wilma said. "We need that trade! If Earth doesn't have an assured, steady flow of food coming in, we face either another holocaust or a long, slow slide toward barbarism."

"Still," Huer persisted, "my apprehension is unrelieved."

"Maybe I can help a little," Wilma volunteered. Dr. Huer stood, listening closely. "Our visit to the Draconian spacecraft may have proved Captain Rogers to be a liar," Wilma said, "but it also proved that the Draconian ship is unarmed, and our scanners picked up no other warcraft within range. The only other ships within striking range were the pirate marauders that attacked while we were up."

"Then you believe it's safe to allow the *Draconia* to penetrate our shield?"

"I believe we can admit the *Draconia* into the Inner City itself. They have no attack craft with enough range to have arrived since we checked out the *Draconia*."

"You don't know how much better you've made me feel," Huer said gratefully.

Aboard the *Draconia* the Princess Ardala posed and preened before her mirror. At a knock on her door and the princess's command of "Enter," Tigerman stepped aside and admitted Kane to the royal chamber. Kane had donned his own fanciest and most elaborate dress uniform, and he advanced to stand behind the preening princess so she could see him as well as herself in her boudoir mirror.

"You are ravishing tonight, my princess," Kane lipped coolly.

"*Your* princess?" Ardala asked suspiciously. "That has the ring of possession to it, Kane."

The uniformed man reached with his arms and folded them around the magnificently outfitted princess. He bent and placed a kiss on the back of her neck. "I was thinking more of a partnership than of possession," he explained.

"Do you truly desire me, Kane?" the princess asked. "Or is it merely my throne that draws you to me?" She disengaged herself from his arms and turned on her dressing-seat to gaze up at him and receive her answer.

"It is *your* desires I serve," Kane said. "I will see to it that one day you will sit on your father's throne as the queen of *all the empire*." With these words Kane bent and kissed the princess directly on the mouth. She permitted him the liberty, then slowly drew away as his demands became greater.

"Conserve your strength, Kane," she commanded. "I'll need your help soon enough. Tomorrow we make our move—the conquest of *Earth!*"

As she broke away from him, Kane said, "Tomorrow, *we* conquer Earth! You could never have reached this point without me, Ardala."

"You truly believe that, don't you, Kane?" The princess's voice was contemptuous of her courtier.

"It is a fact," Kane asserted. "Save for having me at your side, your father would have given this plum to one of your sisters and their warlord husbands. A woman alone, with no husband—to conquer Earth, the greatest prize in all the empire? Never!"

Ardala sneered. "Your ego is your most unattractive feature, Kane, do you know that? There are some things about you that I do admire, but when you start bragging you make me think of sending you to join the stoker gang."

"Learn to love my ego, princess. Don't despise self-appreciation. I will lead you to greatness!"

He paused, then resumed. "Now let us go on. Our friends on earth await their new princess—whether they know it or not!" And he burst into great, ringing peals of strangely frightening laughter.

SEVEN

On the Earth of the twenty-fifth century there were the inner cities and then there was *The Inner City*. Within the Inner City there were chambers and halls, reception rooms and splendid conference parlors and magnificent public buildings of every sort and description. But none could compare with the Palace of Mirrors.

Within the Palace of Mirrors there were splendid chambers and halls of every purpose and sort, each more magnificent and sumptuous than the next, for all of the surviving wealth and all of the surviving glory of earth was represented here. And even so, even within the Palace of Mirrors, there was no chamber to compare even remotely, in dazzling magnificence, with the Grand Ballroom.

The room presented a dazzling vista of immense

chandeliers, glorious, dazzling corruscations of panspectral light that gave the impression that the entire ceiling of the Grand Ballroom was a single, gargantuan, multifaceted lens whose display of ever-shifting illumination never ceased to vary and delight the eye of the beholder.

The walls of the Ballroom were themselves totally mirrored, and the floor was of a material so smooth and reflective and so perfectly finished and polished that it, too, reflected like a single giant mirror.

The effect of being in the room was thus one of being wholly surrounded by, bathed in, permeated and all but absorbed into a supernatural solution of pure light and tone.

Cascades of heraldic banners added slashes of unexpected pattern and tint to the room.

The oval floor drew one's attention to a double-pointed ellipse; at one node of the ellipse stood a raised dais surmounted by a simple, scroll-shaped bench, while at the other stood a similar dais surmounted by the ornately regal throne of the Draconian Realm.

Now there echoed through the great mirrored ballroom the glissandoed cascading notes of heraldic trumpets tuned to a harmony octaves apart. This new Earth of the twenty-fifth century divided its attention, Janus-like, facing to the future and the past at once. Its space-fleets, its ultramodern, domed inner cities, its interstellar trading agreements and supercomputerized technology faced to the future. Its pomp, its heraldry, its ceremony, reminded one and all of the rich heritage of Earth's historic past.

Behind the marching heralds advanced a row of colorfully garbed pages, each carrying a tall, polished standard from which there floated gauzy streamers in heraldic colors. Drummers marched at their flanks, sounding a stately, martial cadence.

Once the heralds, pages, and drummers had completed their ceremonial entry into the ballroom, the official party followed.

Dr. Huer entered first. For once he was not garbed in the informal laboratory tunic that he habitually wore in the performance of his scientific researches. Instead he had adopted a severe, dark-colored outfit of simple line and spartan cut. He ascended the steps of the dais to the plain, scroll-shaped bench.

Now entered Colonel Wilma Deering of the Intercept Squadron, Earth's first and last line of defense. Accompanied by an honor guard of her fellow officers, she had arrayed herself in the full formal dress uniform of a flight colonel of the Third Forces. The effect was breathtaking: at once efficient, military, almost as spartan as the plain dark tunic of Dr. Huer—and yet, through some subtle trick of the tailor's art, through cut, color, fit, texture, and form, she managed to present an appearance dazzlingly feminine, graceful, soft, even in a subtle way erotic. She was the ultimate female warrior, wholly a warrior, yet at the same time wholly female.

A respectful murmur had circled the ballroom at the entrance of Dr. Huer; at that of Colonel Deering, a universal gasp which she chose to acknowledge in no way.

In the foyer of the Grand Ballroom, Buck Rogers stood carefully checking his own appearance before a full-length mirror. He too had arrayed himself in full-dress uniform of captain's rank, but for Buck the pomp and ceremony of the Palace of Mirrors was something to be taken in stride, a mere incident in the progress of the ongoing drama of the Third Directorate of Earth, the Draconian Empire, and the menacing, enigmatic space pirates.

As Buck adjusted the accoutrements of his dress uniform he was observed admiringly by Twiki and Dr. Theopolis. The computer-brain glistened with his own flashing lights and brightly polished exterior. The little drone had been outfitted with a military tunic and stiff collar.

"You look magnificent, Buck," Dr. Theopolis intoned. "But you seem dissatisfied. Is something troubling you?"

"Why did they invite me to this thing?" Buck grumbled. "Nobody believes me anyhow."

"You saved Colonel Deering's life today," Theopolis said. "Not to mention single-handedly fighting off the pirate attack on Princess Ardala's ship.

The princess wants to thank you personally, Buck, aside from everything else."

"Huh!" Buck snorted. "I'd like to have a word or two with the princess, myself. *Alone!*"

"Too bad," Theo's syrupy voice sounded commiseratingly. "I'm afraid that won't be permitted. After all, she's a princess and you're only a low-rated military officer. Even your captaincy is slightly questionable, Buck. What does a United States Air Force commission mean to the Third Force Intercept Squadron?"

Buck ignored Theopolis's words, standing instead deep in thought, hardly even seeing his own image or those of Twiki and Theopolis in the tall mirror. Finally he said, irrelevantly, "Doc, what do you have for a headache. Anything to help?"

"A headache?" Theopolis echoed concernedly. "Are you ill, Buck?"

"I guess I'm still not quite recovered from my long trip," Buck replied, deliberately ambiguous as to which long trip he meant.

"Why didn't you say something, Buck? Twiki will get you a relaxant. You know, most headaches originate with a tension of the neck muscles. But come, it's time to enter the ballroom. We don't want to keep Princess Ardala and her party waiting for us."

Buck straightened his shoulders and marched into the ballroom, Twiki trailing at his heels, Theopolis hanging from the drone's tunic-collared neck.

As Buck entered the Grand Ballroom, Wilma Deering reacted with a curt, silent, but approving nod. Buck bowed formally to her, his movement mirrored by the like-tunicked Twiki.

"That's more like it, captain," Wilma lipped softly. "Now you look like an officer—and a gentleman."

"Doesn't everyone?" Buck replied, eyeing Wilma's costume.

Upon the dais of the scroll-shaped couch, Dr. Huer stood, the focus of a corruscating array of flashing lights. His old-fashioned spectacles reflected the lights but he ignored the effect and held his hand up for silence. Then he began his formal pronouncements of the ceremony.

"Citizens of the Inner City." He gazed around, the focus of all eyes. "At this profound moment in our history, we see hovering in the skies above us an alien vessel. A military spacecraft, a ship of war. As designated spokesman of the Earth Directorate, I have ordered our defenses lowered and our portals opened wide to welcome this awesome visitor, for this is *not* an invader of earth!

"This great war machine has come to us stripped of all weaponry. She is completely unarmed—a shining symbol of peace! Lasting peace—and great goodwill—between the peoples of Earth and of the Draconian Realm."

He looked about him, his lean, drably garbed form suddenly invested with a majesty and strength no glittering uniform could have lent.

"We welcome now the Draconian Trade Delegation under the leadership of the crown heir of the Draconian Realm, her royal highness, the Princess Ardala."

Again the trumpet fanfares with their vibrating glissandoes and the stirring rolls of kettle and snare drums filled the air. From concealed receptacles behind glittering mirrors a shower of fragrant rose petals swirled down. There was a stir in the ornate entryway of the Grand Ballroom, and the assembled throng turned as one person to greet the entrance of the royal entourage.

Now Ardala, flanked by Kane and the ministers of her father's realm, advanced into the ballroom. She was garbed in a stunning, barbarically splendid gown of brocade trimmed with the fur of lynx. She wore a crown of precious metals, trimmed with black glistening fur and encrusted with glittering precious gems of every color. The shape of the crown was that of the ancient Tartar Cap of Monokhash.

The anachronistic combination of barbarism and regal modernity gave her an air like that of a daughter of the great Genghis Khan mixed with that of the Empress Catherine the Great: equally imperious, exotic, breathtakingly beautiful, hot-blooded, passionate—and deadly! She was a smouldering beauty who might at any moment burst into flames of consuming passion!

She swept past aisles of dazzled admirers, climbed unaided to the glittering throne that surmounted the ellipse-node opposite that where Dr. Huer stood, and whirled regally to address the assemblage.

"I bring you greetings on this historic occasion," her throaty, passionate voice rang out. "This occasion which sweeps aside all barriers and opens between us a glorious era of commerce and of peace."

She paused and the assembled dignitaries applauded enthusiastically, silencing themselves only to hear her further comments.

"As proof of his dedication to this pact of commerce and demilitarization, my father the Emperor Draco has sent me to Earth with a glorious surprise for you!"

At the very moment that the Princess Ardala was addressing the assembled dignitaries in the Grand Ballroom of the Palace of Mirrors in earth's Inner City, her immense Draconian flagship was hovering silently above the city's glistening dome.

In the communications room of the *Draconia* the duty officer had been carefully monitoring the ceremony below, receiving every word spoken by means of a small transmitter carried by one of Ardala's courtiers. At the prearranged signal he issued a command to his subordinates: "Stand by to transmit PersonImage—*Now!*"

A crew of technicians cut in a carefully coordinated set of switches and controls.

In the ballroom below, the Princess Ardala had

paused. Now she resumed her speech: "Speaking to you across the immense distances which separate us—I present to you a direct, live PersonImage broadcast from my father, Draco the Conquerer of Space, Warlord of Astrium, Ruler of the Draconian Realm!"

Ardala had delivered her address while standing beside the ornate Draconian throne that had been set up at the node of the elipse. Now, as the air crackled electrically, a holographic image of Draco the Conqueror appeared on the throne itself. The imperial warlord was being seen for the first time by the dignitaries and functionaries of the Third Directorate of Earth. He was a great, fat, barbaric tyrant in the grand manner of Henry the Eighth or Genghis Khan. His voice was deep and rough textured despite all of the electronic filtering to which it was subjected.

The assembly was taken aback for a moment, then politely applauded not the gross and menacing figure that had appeared before them, but the power and the authority that it represented.

"Greetings," Draco intoned sententiously. "I now address you in person, to show you the importance, people of Earth, that I, great Draco, place upon our interplanetary pact."

Draco went on, making grandiose claims and condescendingly generous offers to the people of earth. While the PersonImage spoke to the assembled audience, Kane whispered softly in the ear of the Princess Ardala. "There are two things your father enjoys most," Kane whispered, "spell-binding a crowd and conquering new worlds. This is a rare opportunity for him—to do both at once!"

Ardala's eyes flashed covertly at Kane. "Not Draco," she whispered back, "but *I, Ardala,* shall conquer Earth!"

"With your father's help," Kane grinned wolfishly. "And with mine!" He glanced around the room at the spellbound assemblage. "I wonder what these poor souls would say if they knew the over-stuffed ogre in front of them is a recording and that your father is actually halfway here with his great attack armada!"

While Kane and Ardala carried on their whispered conversation, the PersonImage of the Emperor Draco continued to harangue the attentive crowd. "Here at home in my realm," Draco intoned, "I can only imagine the outpouring of good will from the people of earth to the citizens of the Draconian Empire. Our differences are all behind us now. Before us lies a vista of unending commerce, mutually beneficial trade, cultural exchange and counter-enrichment . . . and eternal peace!"

The fleshy, bejewelled hand seemed to reach into thin air as the living Draco had reached off-camera to receive a document from a bystanding courtier. The hand of the PersonImage reappeared holding an ornately beribboned scroll. "I will now proclaim my royal edict," Draco said. He unrolled the document, held it before him and read portentously from it.

"By my royal command the unarmed spacecraft carrier *Draconia* will descend to the lower atmosphere above the central district of the Inner City. A display of the most sophisticated Draconian technology will be opened to all citizens of Earth's Inner City, and will be known henceforth as the Museum of Interstellar Culture. I do hereby give as my personal gift, to the peaceful peoples of the planet Earth, this undying symbol of peace.

"Thus signed and sealed," the emperor looked up from the document, "by my own hand. Draco, Imperator. Until we meet, then, I bid you farewell."

His jowly face broke into a beaming grin. He waved and nodded at the crowd as if he were actually present and seeing them as they saw him. The crowd cheered in return as trumpet calls and drum rolls resounded.

When the uproar had quieted enough for him to be heard, the dark-tunicked Dr. Huer replied to Princess Ardala as representative of her father the emperor. "On behalf of the Directorate, we accept with pleasure this great gift from your father the emperor." The old man bowed low to the smiling princess while the audience again resumed its applause and cheers.

"Let the celebration begin!" Dr. Huer proclaimed loudly.

And now the crowd separated itself into strictly dictated court formations as the music of trumpets and drums was replaced by stately, formal orches-

tral harmonies. The court formation was that of
the formal ceremonial dances of the twenty-fifth
century. It was a mixture, like the rest of Earth's
culture in this era, of the forward-looking and the
nostalgic, the futuristic and the antique. It contained mixtures of the minuet and the quadrille,
the formal ballet and the free-form expressive
dance.

The partners met, bowed, curtsied, circled, separated and reassembled in stately formality. A new
touch was the passing of delicately lighted globes
of the most fragile glass from hand to hand among
the dancers. Within each swayed a delicate candle,
and when the great chandeliers were dimmed at
the climax of the dance, the Grand Ballroom was
transformed into a fairyland where multicolored
fireflies floated on graceful, rhythmic breezes that
wafted invisibly through midnight glades.

At the apex of the parade of the fairylamps the
Princess Ardala stood, a figure of breathtaking
barbaric beauty, a new Titania receiving the
chaste, formal kisses of fealty from the dignitaries
who moved in stately rhythm past the throne of
Draconia.

Yet even as Ardala received the formal tribute
of the waiting dignitaries, her eye probed the
ballroom before her.

And at the opposite end of the ballroom, observing with a keen appreciation of the symbolism as
well as the immediate beauty of the spectacle,
stood Buck Rogers.

For an instant Ardala's eye caught that of Buck. She seemed to transmit a jolt of human electricity across the ballroom to the earthman, and in return he nodded to her, smiling seriously. The princess caught the expression, returned it with the subtlest hint of some added ingredient.

The line continued to move past the princess, while Buck's attention was caught by an insistent tapping at his leg. He looked down and saw Twiki and Dr. Theopolis standing, the drone holding something toward him in one metallic hand. "We brought you a quantity of Nirvana, Buck," Dr. Theopolis said.

"Eh?" Buck expressed complete puzzlement.

"For your headache," Theopolis explained. "Nirvana is a very strong relaxant. You take a single capsule, that should relieve any tension that is causing your headache. More than one would make you very woozy, though, so be careful with the medicine."

"Thanks," Buck said. He took the little bottle of capsules and tucked it into his tunic. "One more thing, guys. I need a rose."

"Did you say, *rose?*" Theopolis asked.

"A red one."

"I don't understand, Buck. Why do you need a rose?"

"Never mind, Theopolis, Twiki. Just get me one, please, quickly!"

"Just a minute, Twiki." Dr. Theopolis spoke authoritatively, stopping the quad in its tracks.

"Buck is getting us involved in something here, and before we commit ourselves I'd like to find out just what he's planned."

Twiki squealed characteristically and began to move again.

"Wait, wait," Theopolis's voice rose with agitation, "where are you taking me, Twiki?"

As the two mechanical beings departed, Wilma Deering approached Buck Rogers, her appearance of restrained poise and trim attractiveness a telling contrast to the overwhelmingly barbaric beauty of the Princess Ardala. "How did you like the presentation, Captain Rogers?" Wilma asked Buck.

"Impressive," Buck commented. "Did that light-show come all the way from her daddy's kingdom?"

"I don't understand your terms of almost contemptuous familiarity Captain." Wilma frowned sternly, then continued. "I would suggest a more respectful form of reference than *daddy*. The Emperor Draco may well be the greatest leader that this galaxy has ever known."

"He *is* impressive," Buck conceded. But the expression on his face and the gesture he made with his hands, indicating King Draco's imposing girth, suggested that Buck was still not taking the leader with total seriousness—or at any rate, was far from awed by the imperial Draconian presence.

Before Wilma could reply, Buck continued, "I

wonder why Draco didn't come in person. Or do peaceful conquests bore him?"

"Conquests? You'd better get your understanding of the treaty squared away, Captain Rogers. This is a mutual trade pact concluded between equals."

"Uh huh!" Buck grunted ironically. "And the princess up there and her boyfriend Kane are just a couple of down-home folks, doin' their jobs and ekin' out a livin'. Is that it?"

"I think we all know why you resent their presence," Wilma replied coldly. "It spells the finish of you and your pirate pals, Rogers!"

"A word of advice, Colonel," Buck replied with equal remoteness. "Beware of Greeks bearing gifts."

A look of real puzzlement crossed Wilma's face. "Greeks?" she repeated. "What are Greeks?"

"I guess it's pretty far back now," Buck explained. "You folks have apparently lost most of Earth's history. Do you remember the story of the Trojan Horse?"

"Is that some kind of sign of the zodiac?" Wilma asked.

"Never mind." Buck shook his head hopelessly. "Forget all about it. I guess I come from a time that was hopelessly paranoid. See ya around."

He started to walk away just as Twiki and Theopolis returned from the mission upon which he had sent them. Twiki carefully balanced a satin pillow in his arms. A perfect red rose with tiny dew drops sparkling on its petals reposed on the pillow.

As the drone scuttered up, Wilma said sternly, "I thought I told you to stay with him. There's definitely something not right with that man, and I want to find out what it is!"

"He isn't feeling well tonight, Wilma dear," Theopolis intoned.

"He looks like he feels all right to me. Hmph!" She stood with her fists balled on her hips as she looked into the distant crowd where Buck had disappeared. Finally she turned her eyes back to the mechanicals and noticed the pillow and rose for the first time. "What's that for?" Wilma demanded.

"We don't know," Theopolis replied. "It's just something that Buck asked for. He seems to be up to—Twiki, stop!" As the drone scuttered away again Theopolis called back to Wilma, "I don't know what's got into Twiki tonight. He seems to have developed a mind of his own all of a sudden!" Theopolis blinked his lights furiously. "Twiki, you're at it again. Twiki, stop, where are you going this time? We can't run away from Wilma like this, Twiki!"

But Twiki was scuttling determinedly toward the reception line where Buck Rogers was standing in place, impatiently awaiting his turn to be presented to the princess. The little quad scuttled up to Buck and lifted the satin pillow toward him, presenting the red rose for his approval.

"What kept you, Twiki?" Buck asked. "Here, let me have that."

Dr. Theopolis flashed his lights. "Buck, no one else is giving flowers to the princess. You're going to make everyone else in the hall look—"

"Stick close, fellas," Buck interrupted. "We're in the on-deck circle." He waited while the man ahead of him in line, a pompous, middle-aged bureaucrat with a twittering, overweight wife on his elbow, was presented to Princess Ardala.

Then it was Buck's turn.

He drew back his shoulders and stepped into position before the princess. Ardala responded to Buck's splendid appearance and to the force of personality that she felt radiating from him. Her lovely, subtly tilted eyes—what the poet-bard of an earlier age would have poesied as her downward-slanting eyes—glowed under long, curved lashes that were both delicate—and cruel.

Ardala extended her hand in formal greeting. At the same time she spoke to Buck. "Congratulations to you, Captain Rogers. And may I offer my imperial thanks. We are grateful to you for saving the *Draconia* from plunder by those horrible privateers."

"Not too loudly, princess," Buck answered. "Around here, they seem to think that I'm a privateer myself. Thanks to you!"

"Thanks to me?" the princess asked in surprise. Buck tried without success to tell whether her expression represented mockery or real astonishment, or some combination of the two. "I hope I didn't cause you any embarrassment," the princess continued. "You aren't angry with me, are you?"

"Does this look like I'm angry?" Buck snapped his fingers at the robot by his side. Twiki raised the rose-bearing pillow to Ardala as Theopolis intoned in his syrupy tones, "On behalf of the people and the government of—"

Buck took the rose from its satin repository and handed it to Ardala. "From me to you," he said simply.

Beside the mirrored wall of the ballroom, Wilma angrily observed Buck's intimacy with the royal guest of honor. Wilma's heart was a seething cauldron of mixed emotions: attraction to Buck, jealousy of Ardala, anger with the man for paying attention to the princess rather than to herself. She was realizing that her own feelings were complex and difficult—and that the difficulty swirled maddeningly around the vortex of William Rogers!

Wilma saw Ardala take the rose greedily from Buck, clearly aware that it was not merely a beautiful flower but a symbol of triumph in the contest for his attention. She lifted the rose to her nostrils and sniffed eagerly. Kane at her side snarled silently. The princess glanced down at the robot and the brain.

"And who is your charming little friend?" Ardala asked Buck.

"His name is Twiki," Dr. Theopolis volunteered.

"And that thing around his neck," Buck added,

"is Dr. Theopolis, former member of the Inner City Council of Computers."

Twiki bowed, Theopolis dangling from his tunic.

"Your majesty," Theopolis intoned.

"May I have the honor of the next dance?" Buck asked Ardala.

Jealously, Kane put in, "The princess does not—"

"Does not mind if she does," Ardala interrupted him. She reached for Buck's arm, took it and descended at his side, from the throne-bearing dais to the gleamingly polished dance floor. The crowd parted to permit them room as Buck and Ardala made their way to a position near the orchestra. At a signal from Buck, given over the shapely shoulder of Princess Ardala, the orchestra began once more to play.

Wilma Deering, watching this show, frowned angrily. No, for all that she had virtually dismissed Buck from her presence, grading him as a boor at best and a traitor at worst, she was not in the least pleased to see him moving on intimate terms with the Princess Ardala.

While Buck carried on his odd triangular relationship with Ardala and Wilma, Dr. Huer and Kane had left the Grand Ballroom and were conferring on serious matters outside. Their setting was a beautiful balcony, beneath which the vista of the Inner City presented a breathtaking view. But neither Huer nor Kane was interested in the sight. Both were concerned with what information they could obtain—and what information or misinformation, they might be called upon to provide to the other.

"I must say that I owe you a debt of gratitude, Kane," Dr. Huer said in his dry, old man's voice. "Or perhaps more accurately, I should say that this entire planet owes you a debt. You know, there are those who consider you a traitor to the world of your birth for giving up your Earth citizenship and becoming a subject of the Emperor Draco."

"A traitor—me?" Kane burst into raucous laughter. "Surely you're not serious!"

"I definitely am. But they must all see by now that you have been our friend at court. It was your efforts that made this trade treaty possible for Earth and Draconia."

"We have all worked, Dr. Huer. It's been hard, I'll admit."

"If the Council were so to honor you, Kane, would you consider resuming your Earth citizenship?"

"Nothing would suit me more! I must say that I've missed the Inner City. Draconia has its splendors, but you know, Doctor, once you grow up in a place. . . ." Kane pointed across the vista before them. "That building over there—it was the Communications Center when I was a boy. I wonder, is it still?"

Huer nodded. "And the Department of Water

and Power is now in the copper tower over to the left." He raised a dark-tunicked sleeve and pointed.

Kane grunted. "It's been so long, Doc, so long. Sometimes I can't even remember. For instance, the central security barracks and the Intercept Squadron launching bays—they used to be concealed on the north side. Least I think I recall that. Are they still over there?"

Huer hesitated, smiling a secret smile. "That would be secret information, Kane. Not that I distrust you personally, of course. I'm sure you'll understand."

Kane smiled back, showing rows of massive, grinning teeth. The two men resembled a black bear and a pink flamingo as they stood side by side. But he knew that Huer's power lay in his brilliant brain, not his spare body, just as Huer knew that Kane's strength lay not in his massively muscled bulk, powerful though that body was, but in his influence with the Princess Ardala and through her the mighty empire that her father Draco ruled.

"Sure," Kane laughed at last, "I understand. Besides, what difference does it make where a few troopers keep their foot-lockers, eh, Doc? Besides," and he smiled again, less menacingly than the last time, "I'll always be an earthman at heart, regardless of what my citizenship papers say. Maybe I'll just stay on Earth this time, permanently."

"I do hope so," Huer agreed.

They shared a last glance at the city's vista, then returned to the Grand Ballroom where the orchestra was still performing its courtly, formalized, modern-archaic dance-music.

"Is this the way they dance where you come from?" Buck asked Ardala as she swayed formally in his arms.

"With slight variations," she replied. "The universal culture of this space age, you know."

"Huh! You'll have to forgive me then, Ardala. My dancing is about five hundred years out of date."

"If you've another preference," the princess replied, "you know, this *is* my party."

Buck turned to the orchestra leader and snapped his fingers to get the musician's attention. When he had done so he continued to pop his knuckles, setting up a rocking rhythm that he'd learned in the remote era of the twentieth century. He moved like a famous disco dancer of the ancient past. The orchestra leader, the musicians, the dancers, and not least by any means, the Princess Ardala, gaped as Buck demonstrated a sexy boogie step of the late 1980s.

"What are you doing?" Ardala asked at last.

"Gettin' down," Buck answered. "It's from before your time, princess. Hope it doesn't frighten you."

"Frighten me?" she answered sharply. "*Nothing* frightens me!"

"Great," Buck encouraged her. "Then why don't you give it a try. It ain't hard to do, lady, just lay back and boogie."

Princess Ardala joined Buck in the boogie step, at first hesitantly, then with more confidence, finally with a barbaric abandon that brought an admiring gleam to his blue eyes. He even began to hum a familiar tune along with the orchestra's beat. "Chicago, Chicago. . . ."

The onlookers stood in awe. Wilma had come to the edge of the crowd and stood watching Buck and Ardala. Her face showed that she was utterly appalled by the abandon of the public performance. Theopolis and Twiki stood beside Wilma.

"It's expressive," Theopolis declared, his lights flashing in time to the emphatic rhythm.

"It's disgusting," Wilma sneered.

"Primeval," Theopolis said.

"I do not approve," Wilma said, adopting a regal tone more appropriate to the wildly dancing Ardala.

All the while that Buck and Ardala had been dancing, Twiki had watched and listened, his mechanical circuits and relays clicking over in time to the music. Now he tried a few steps of his own in imitation of Captain Rogers.

"Twiki, stop that! People are watching!" Theopolis scolded.

172

Instead of stopping, Twiki squeaked his pleasure and increased the vigor of his steps.

Meanwhile, Buck and Ardala carried on a breathless conversation while they danced before the hard-working orchestra.

"What happens if you bump together?" Ardala asked.

"You're automatically man and wife," Buck replied sardonically.

"You're quite a man, Captain Rogers," Ardala replied. She shifted her position to move closer to him as she continued her steps. "I suppose the Earth people believe your incredible fairy tale about being frozen for five hundred years."

"Not on your life!" Buck denied. "They think I'm a spy!"

"A spy?" Ardala laughed wildly, her head thrown back and her lush, dark hair cascading across her sensuous shoulders and down her smooth, graceful back. "A spy!" she repeated. "One of mine?"

"They aren't sure," Buck said. "Yours—or the pirates."

"How would you like to join up?" Ardala asked. "Might as well be hanged for a sheep as for a lamb, Captain!"

"Who do I see to make my move?" Buck asked.

The princess moved even closer to him, raised her painted lips to Buck's ear and hissed a single syllable. "Me!"

173

Beside Twiki and Theopolis, Wilma watched in fury and confusion. "Is anything wrong?" the computer-brain asked. "You look upset, Wilma, my dear."

"I ordered you to keep Captain Rogers out of trouble," Wilma told the computer angrily.

"I'm sorry, Wilma," Theopolis's lights blinked a blushing crimson, "he just seems to have a way of getting into things before we can get him out."

"Yes, I can see that!" Wilma snapped.

As Wilma turned her back and stalked angrily from the room, Buck caught a glimpse of her over Ardala's shoulder. He said nothing of the incident to Ardala, but his thoughts, like Wilma's, were confused. Buck saw Wilma pass Kane on her way from the hall. Kane proceeded across the dance floor, ignoring the powerful rhythm of the music and striding determinedly up to the dancing couple.

"Your highness," Kane demanded.

Ardala, still caught up in the power of the dance but tossing a glance back to Kane, said, "What is it?"

"Your highness—some of the ministers would like a few minutes of your time. It's important, your highness."

"Later, Kane." Ardala returned her full attention to the music and to Buck.

"Business of the realm cannot wait," Kane insisted. "I'm sorry, your highness, but your duty must outweigh trivial personal dalliances." He cast a contemptuous sneer at Buck.

Ardala whirled furiously toward Kane. "Don't you order me around, you pig," she hissed in a hate-filled voice.

Kane leaned forward, spoke in a low tone but with urgency that compelled even the outraged Ardala to pay attention. "Your father expects you to serve the best interests of the realm, Ardala! You'd better remember, if you fail, Draco has twenty-nine other daughters!"

Ardala made a low, animal growl in her throat. Her eyes flashed and she raised her long, talonlike fingernails as if she intended to rake Kane's face with them. She had actually started toward him, claws extended, when she felt Buck Rogers's hand on her wrist. She turned, snarling, toward Buck, then got control of herself and pulled back from Kane.

The courtier stood before her, his normally swarthy complexion pallid for once. He had escaped by the narrowest of margins a public humiliation unparalleled in his career. If Ardala had clawed his face he would not have dared retaliate here in the Grand Ballroom before the assembled dignitaries of Earth and of Draconia. He would have had no choice but to submit to a public scourging and then withdraw in disgrace.

Instead, Ardala turned toward Buck and repeated a polite formula through angry, clenched teeth. "It's been a great pleasure, Captain Rogers. But it seems that we both have our duty cut out for us."

She extended her hand, those deadly talons now turned harmlessly down. Buck Rogers took the extended hand, courteously kissed it, murmured *sotto voce*, "Later, perhaps, Ardala?"

"I depart aboard my private launch at midnight, to return to the *Draconia*." Her eyes met those of the dashing earthman, full of unspoken promise.

The princess turned, took Kane's arm demandingly and ascended to rejoin her ministers who awaited beside her throne. Her bodyguard, Tigerman, watched all of this, the thoughts behind those inscrutable slitted eyes a mystery to all save himself.

Buck Rogers snapped a brittle wisecrack at Tigerman and strode away from the ellipse, headed toward the balcony outside the ballroom where Kane and Huer had conducted their earlier exchange. This time Buck found Wilma Deering standing there, alone, her eyes gazing sadly out over the beautiful, gleaming spires and shafts of the Inner City.

Buck approached Wilma from behind and spoke softly. "It's a very beautiful sight, in its own way. We had city skylines in my era, Wilma, some of them breathtaking to behold. But the Inner City is unique."

Wilma's reply was so soft as to be nearly inaudible, yet it dripped icicles to the hearer. "I would much prefer to be alone just now. If you please, Captain Rogers."

Buck heard his name accompanied by a little sound, a sound that Wilma nearly, but not quite, managed to suppress. The sound might have been a gasp—or a sob.

"Okay," Buck said, "I'm sorry. So long." He turned away and started back toward the Grand Ballroom.

"Wait!" Wilma cried. Buck stopped in his tracks, waiting for Wilma. "I'm sorry," she echoed Buck's earlier words.

"For what?" He turned to face her again. "Sorry for wanting to be alone? It's good for you. A little solitude, helps you get your thoughts in order. Not five hundred years of it, maybe, but—"

"Don't try to make me feel better, please. I've behaved very badly. It's just that I'm so very mixed up." She raised one hand to her brow. As she did so, Buck couldn't help noticing the contrast between Wilma's fingernails, gracefully rounded but trimmed short so as not to interfere with the operation of her Starfighter up in orbit, and the dark, pointed talons of the Draconian princess.

Buck shook his head. "I'm not quite myself either."

"At least you have an excuse," Wilma said. "That is, you do, if you're—if you're—"

"Telling the truth?" he supplied.

"You see?" Wilma said. A tear at last fell from one eye, landed with the tiniest of splashes on the form-fitting bodice of her trim military tunic. "Oh, Buck, I'm only making it worse." She stopped again, clutched one hand with the other and forced herself to breath deeply. "This is very difficult, Captain Rogers," she resumed. "I am a commander. I am not in the habit of explaining my—my—emotions."

"Take your time," Buck offered.

Wilma drew herself up, inhaled deeply and began. "It may not really help, Buck. You know, I've been trained all my life to be a leader. I couldn't have elected a less demanding role. But in the National Sensitivity Tests, my score was a nine in Dominance. So it was natural for me to enter the military as a career.

"You see, Flight Officers are expected to go by the book. We are expected never to let personal feelings enter the equation. So if I'm clumsy and can't express this correctly, I hope you'll be patient with me."

Buck checked his watch unobtrusively. Ardala's launch would be taking off for its return flight to the *Draconia* soon.

"I'll try to be brief," Wilma said. She looked up into Buck's blue-eyed countenance, then turned slowly to lean on the parapet and gaze out over the Inner City as she spoke. "I've never experienced feelings like this in my entire career, Buck. I've found myself laughing. Then crying. Furiously angry with you. Then overflowing with remorse and—and—tenderness for you. I did think you

178

were a spy, Captain Rogers. But I know now that I was wrong."

She took her hands from the parapet, turned and looked up at Buck, moving closer to him as she did. "I could never have fallen in love with a spy, I know that. And yet, I've fallen in love!"

At these words Buck was astonished. Before he could respond in any way, Wilma had reached up and drawn his face down to her own, and kissed him tenderly on the mouth. After a little bit she drew back and asked, "Did you like that?"

Buck blinked. "It was first class," he said.

"Then I did it correctly?" Wilma asked.

"Really outstanding."

"Thank you," she said softly.

"You're welcome as all get out," Buck told her.

"Then why don't we go someplace," Wilma said. "The Palace of Mirrors is so public."

Buck checked his watch again. "I'd really love to, Wilma, but it *is* getting late and I'm a little tired." He saw the hurt expression on her face. "I've been out of it for five hundred years," he added. "So I think I'd better go easy on reentry."

He leaned over and kissed her softly on the cheek.

"You're leaving!" Wilma exclaimed. "Just like that!"

"Just for tonight, colonel. We'll get back to this later on, I promise." He tossed her a casual salute and made for the nearest exit.

Wilma stared after him unbelievingly. For a few seconds her expression was one of deep hurt. Then the hurt was transformed into white-hot anger.

EIGHT

^^^

Princess Ardala gazed around the Grand Ballroom, still filled with swirling dancers, swaying musicians, glittering courtiers and dignitaries of the Draconian Empire and the Earth Directorate. The hour was late but the festive occasion would continue as long as its honored luminary the princess cared to have it do so.

When she felt that enough time had passed the princess discreetly signaled the orchestra leader and the music switched to the melody traditionally associated with the end of a formal gala. The leader of the Earth delegation, the aged Dr. Huer, ascended Princess Ardala's dais to bid her goodnight.

He bent and kissed her hand. Then he made a circle of the dignitaries, exchanging a formal farewell and a handclasp with each. Even when he reached towering Tigerman, Huer raised his hand halfway. Tigerman made a deep, rumbling growl, perhaps his equivalent of a polite greeting.

"Er, yes. Well, and good evening and, er, pleasant dreams to you, too," Dr. Huer mumbled. "Or, ah, good hunting. Catch a mousie or whatever one wishes a, ah, creature of your sort."

Tigerman raised one murderously clawed paw.

Dr. Huer gingerly pressed his fragile old hand against the creature's rasping pads, then withdrew.

The Princess Ardala cast a final glance around the ballroom, hoping to spot Buck Rogers in the still-colorful throng. She failed to find him and heaved a disappointed sigh as she drew her cloak around her regal shoulders.

She threw her head back regally and descended from the dais, her richly trimmed cloak drawn about her, Tigerman at her elbow, her ministers and courtiers trailing behind in an order rigidly determined by official protocol. Prominent among them, jealous of his place in the line and eager as ever to move forward to the princess's side, was the oily Kane.

They made their way, accompanied by an Intercept Squadron honor guard, to the princess's private launch. As soon as they had boarded safely and found their proper positions, the launch streaked upward, headed from Earth's glittering Inner City to the Emperor Draco's great flagship *Draconia*.

Inside the cabin of the launch, Ardala was seated on a remarkable piece of furniture, a cross between a purely functional launch couch and a regal throne. The strap that ran across her graceful lap was another example of the same sort of compromise between function and symbolism. It was richly tooled in patterns derived from the royal crest of Draconia, studded with sparkling gems of every color. And it was a safety belt.

Above the princess's head twin tiny speakers hung on wires so fine as to be invisible, providing musical distraction for her highness during the tedium of flight. Ardala gazed from the launch, watching the stars of the earthly sky, moving her head slightly in time with the music as if reliving a moment of the ball just ended. To either side of her throne-couch the launch's bulkheads were covered with the richest spotted animal pelts, hung with the crest and arms of Imperial Draconia.

Suddenly the pleasant, soothing music was interrupted. Ardala reached for a control panel to correct the malfunction, but before she could reach the switch a new, yet familiar, voice came over the twin speakers mounted on their invisible wires.

"Chicago, Chicago," the voice sang merrily.

Ardala swung her head around to see where the singing was coming from. The curtain that cut off the galley from the royal cabin was drawn aside and Buck Rogers entered the room. He was singing his old-fashioned song, carrying a tray in both hands with a bottle of Vinol on it and two elaborate goblets.

Tigerman leaped to his feet, snarling, placing himself between Princess Ardala and the earthman Buck Rogers.

"It's all right," Ardala soothed Tigerman. He cropped his menace from a snarl to a low, rumbling growl but continued slowly to advance toward Buck.

"Listen to her, fella," Buck urged. "She's making sense. Take it easy. It really is okay."

"I invited Captain Rogers to join me," Ardala said.

Tigerman halted and turned a curious look upon the princess. Never before had a stranger appeared in the royal cabin, and his lifelong conditioning had been to kill, if need be to die, in defense of his mistress. But if she herself said that this earthman was an invited, if unexpected, guest, then it must be all right.

He returned to his place beside the royal launch-couch and curled up on the floor, for all the world like a thousand-pound housecat curled up by his mistress's easy chair.

"This is state business," Princess Ardala told her bodyguard. "As soon as we arrive you will escort

184

us to the royal stateroom and post yourself in the corridor to see that we are not disturbed."

"That's right," Buck agreed. "In the corridor. *Outside* the princess's door."

Tigerman lifted one tawny eyebrow and glared at Buck from out of one yellow slitted eye.

Meanwhile, behind the curtain in the launch's galley, a cupboard door sprung open revealing the sanitary, stainless-steel interior of the storage area. In the midst of the racks and shelves of shipboard food supplies stood a three-foot-tall metal drone and, slung around his neck, lights flashing the colors of the spectrum, a super-advanced computer-brain.

With a quick glance around, the little quad scuttered out of the cupboard and stood in the middle of the galley.

"We're almost there," Dr. Theopolis's soothing, low voice said. "Twiki, where you going now? I know that it was chilly there in the cupboard, but we have little choice, you know. Our orders were to stick close to Buck and keep him out of trouble. He may need us at any time. So back into the cupboard, let's go. Twiki, I'm speaking to you!"

The quad shook his head and squealed.

"Oh, I know there are refrigeration coils in that cupboard," Theopolis said. "It can't be helped. After all, that's how the Draconians preserve their food."

Twiki hugged himself, opened another cupboard—this one not refrigerated—and withdrew a bottle from it. He opened the bottle and took a drink.

"All right," Theopolis said. "It's too bad there isn't room for us in that cupboard. But a little Vinol will keep your circuits from freezing when we go back where we came from. All right now, I suppose we can take the bottle with us. Back into the cooler."

Twiki edged back into the refrigerated cupboard, shivering, Theopolis around his neck, the Vinol bottle in his metal hand.

While the royal launch arrowed upward from earth, a brief conversation took place back in the Inner City. Its participants were Colonel Wilma Deering of the Third Force Intercept Squadron and the aged Dr. Huer, chairman of the Earth Directorate.

"Any word?" Wilma Deering fretted, hoping that Huer would have some information for her.

"I'm afraid not," Huer replied. "We've searched the entire Intercept Squadron base and all adjacent sectors of the Inner City. Captain Rogers is simply nowhere to be found!"

"Oh, what did I expect?" Wilma asked bitterly. "What should I ever have expected from a primitive who came to us from half a thousand years in the past, before the great holocaust even took place?"

"Don't blame yourself, child," Huer said. "I

shall go and see if there's any word at all." Huer left the room.

Alone, Wilma paced the room, fuming. Finally she picked up a miniature statuette that stood on a little pedestal all its own and hurled it furiously into what appeared to be a roaring fireplace. The fire and the fireplace were nothing but a TV simulation, and the impact of the heavy statuette shattered the screen into a million tinkling fragments.

"You are a spy, Buck Rogers!" Wilma almost shouted. "You were never anything but a double agent, and I know exactly where you've gone to now!"

Suddenly Wilma began to sob in a most uncolonel-like manner.

And aboard the flagship *Draconia* the royal launch had docked with absolute precision and its occupants debarked into the spacious landing bay of the great starship.

The Princess Ardala and Captain Buck Rogers made their way through corridors, past bowing guards and Draconian troopers, to the princess's royal stateroom. They entered, accompanied by Ardala's guardian Tigerman. The princess turned and commanded Tigerman with a single sharp word, "Out!"

The giant bodyguard growled menacingly at Buck but obeyed. Ardala reached and slammed the door behind him. She clicked a latch into place.

"There. Now we will be undisturbed," she gloated.

Buck looked around him. The magnificent state-room glowed with indirect lighting. The sumptuous, semibarbaric style of the Draconian Realm at its most self-indulgent was apparent, giving the room a romantically anachronistic suggestion of some regal chamber in the ziggurats of ancient Babylon or the palaces of Macchu Pichu.

"I bet that Tigerman would make a better pet if you'd have him fixed," Buck wisecracked.

Ardala registered a smirk at the jibe, then moved behind her privacy screen. In a moment Buck saw the royal cloak flung over the top of the screen.

"Pour yourself a drink while I slip into something more comfortable," Ardala's voice came from the other side of the screen.

"Nothing has changed," Buck muttered, "Five hundred and four years and they're still slipping into something more comfortable. Oh well. . . ."

He located the Vinol in an ornate side-cabinet near the princess's bed, lifted the bottle from its place and poured two goblets of the sparkling liquid. From the waistband of his tunic he extracted the vial of headache pills that Theopolis and Twiki had fetched for him during the gala at the Grand Ballroom in the Palace of Mirrors. He removed several of the tiny tablets and dropped them carefully into one of the goblets. Each pill, as it struck the Vinol, blossomed into a miniature fountain of bubbles and foam, then subsided, leaving the Vinol appearing exactly as it had before.

"You're in for a little surprise, Ardala," Buck said.

From behind the screen Ardala called back, "You mustn't peek, now, Captain."

"Bear with me, Princess," Buck replied. "You know, it's been over five hundred years."

"I hope I don't disappoint then, all the more," Ardala said. She swept from behind the screen wearing a boudoir gown the likes of which Buck had never even imagined. Her dress possessed the outward appearance of thoughtless casualness that Buck in his inner recesses knew must actually be the most studied purposefulness.

While he appreciated the effect of the gown, Buck was too preoccupied with his mission to be swept away by the beautiful temptations the princess offered.

Now came the hardest part. How to lead the lovely Ardala to drink the doctored Vinol before things got out of hand. Buck decided to play as straight as he could.

He gaped.

"Have you nothing to say?" Ardala demanded.

Buck made his voice sound as if he was profoundly affected by the performance. "I-uh. Princess Ardala, you don't know what you can do to the weak heart of a man who's five hundred twenty-eight years old!" He caught his breath. "Until this moment, I'd kind of forgotten what I've been missing since 1987."

"Well then—I, too have a confession to make," Ardala crooned.

Ardala moved slowly toward him. "It's that—I hadn't realized what *I'd* been missing, either! You're different, Captain Rogers—different from the kind of men I'm accustomed to knowing. Ardala's voice had changed subtly. Now there was a note of pleading creeping into her silken tones.

"A princess of the realm pretty much has her way, you know. For a while that's very pleasant, but after enough of it she wants a man who is—more manly. Like you. You're arrogant. You flagrantly disregard orders, from me as well as from anyone else."

Buck was sitting on the edge of Ardala's bed, not by his own choice but because there was nowhere else to sit in the room. At that moment Buck felt sorry for the princess. Though young and beautiful, the awful power to which she was heiress made her a sad, lonely figure in this drama of interstellar politics and intrigue.

Ardala came and knelt in the exotic animal-fur rug beside the bed, placing her hands on his uniformed legs. She looked up into his face, emotion filling her features. "Buck Rogers," she whispered passionately, "you are the kind of man who could unseat my father. You could place yourself on the throne of Draconia, with me at your side as Empress of the Realm."

"You may not believe this," Buck said, "but your father's seat is the farthest thing from my mind at this moment, Ardala."

"I brought you here for a reason," the princess breathed.

"I was counting on it," Buck countered.

"I want you at my side, Buck Rogers!"

Buck said nothing, stunned for a moment by her brazen declaration of intent.

"Consider it," Ardala said seriously. "You don't know what it's like to be the daughter of Draco the Conqueror—with twenty-nine sisters nipping at your heels. With weaseling courtiers like that pig Kane clawing at you for power.

"But with a real man like you, Buck Rogers, I could sweep aside Kane and the others. I could defy my father, lead my own life. And think of our children! What a magnificent dynasty we would found!"

"Children? Dynasty? Aren't we getting a little ahead of ourselves?" Buck asked.

"There isn't much time," Ardala said.

Buck's brow wrinkled with concentration at that. Ardala, clearly, was on the verge of making an important revelation of some sort. He prompted her to continue.

Ardala removed one of her hands from Buck's shoulders and reached for a glass of Vinol. Perhaps she felt the need of a drink, perhaps it was some new pose, perhaps the gesture was just a play for time while she planned out her next move and her next sentence. Whatever the case, her move gave Buck the opportunity he'd awaited.

Buck held a glass toward the princess, carefully ascertaining that it was the one containing the Vinol he had doctored with the tablets from the little bottle in his tunic.

"We have to be very careful," Ardala said.

"We do?" Buck echoed. "Why? Careful of what?"

Ardala sipped carefully from her glass. "Our timing is not what I would have preferred."

Buck grinned wryly. "Like I said, nothing ever changes."

Ardala leaned forward, pressing her lips warmly onto Buck's. "Why couldn't I have met you sooner?" she asked passionately.

Buck shook his head. "We have plenty of time left—don't we?"

She pressed forward, kissed him again, more fervently than before. She struggled to her feet, drained her glass at a single breath and threw it across the room against the wall where it shattered with a crash and fell to the floor in a pile of tinkling fragments.

She whirled and stumbled back to the bed. She tumbled onto the massed furs there, sprawling face-down amidst the deep-piled luxurious pelts. "What—what am I doing?" she asked drunkenly.

"Never mind that," Buck soothed her. "You're doing everything just fine. Believe me, I'd tell you if you weren't."

She lifted her head, turned to face Buck. He watched her with calm detachment. Her movements were slower, less perfectly coordinated, as she tried to encircle him in her arms.

"I barely know you," Ardala crooned, "how could I have become so desperate? So—"

Buck interrupted her, leaning over and pushing her gently but firmly back down onto the bed.

Ardala looked blearily at Buck. Her eyes were glazed, her breath coming in short gasps. She struggled to speak. "Buck, I feel so—I don't know. It's pleasant too, but— but—"

"That's funny," Buck said. "I feel bright-eyed and bushy-tailed."

"You're not used to this bed," Ardala said.

"It's a very nice bed," Buck returned. "But not so unusual that I can see."

"No, you don't understand," Ardala went on. "It's computerized. It has an electronic mattress. It has sensors that attune its firmness to every contour of the body."

"Back in the old days, machines knew their places," Buck commented sardonically.

"No, our way is more efficient," Ardala quarreled.

"Such things require a human touch," Buck insisted.

Ardala tried to push herself upright, slipped back. "Oh, Buck, I'm so drowsy. Won't you turn off the lights so I can rest."

Buck reached for a control switch and darkened the stateroom. He reached for Ardala and she responded in a half-awake, half-asleep languor. "Buck, Buck," she breathed.

"What is it?"

"If you're a spy, Buck, you know I'll have to have you killed. I'd hate to do that. You're so nice, Buck. But I *will* have you killed if you're a spy."

"Now that," commented Buck as he rolled over in the great fur-covered bed, "is some of the nicest pillowtalk I've ever heard, Ardala."

He reached for her once more and in the darkness he could feel her going limp and slack. The doctored Vinol had taken its toll. Princess Ardala lay sound asleep across the great fur-covered mattress. Even though she was far beyond awakening by a mere sound, Buck instinctively moved with a minimum of noise or disturbance as he climbed quickly from the bed.

And in another section of the *Draconia* Kane sat in the command seat gazing down at the Inner City of earth. The *Draconia* was in a synchronous orbit above the shimmering dome, revolving freely over the earth, falling freely in a sense, yet moving so that its twenty-four-hour revolution about the earth matched the planet's twenty-four-hour period of rotation. The effect was as if the ship were anchored in space directly above the Inner City.

"Look at them down there. Sleeping! The fools will never know what hit them."

The Inner City itself, beneath its shimmering protective dome, resembled a sea of diamonds laid out on a jeweler's cloth of blackest velvet.

In the starship, a technician addressed himself to Kane. "Stand by to receive classified transmission from the armada," the technician stated. "Carrier wave is activated and preliminary image pattern is forming, sir."

Kane jumped from the command seat as if it had suddenly grown white hot. In the seat he had vacated, the gross form of the Emperor Draco, resplendent in the decorated uniform of the Supreme Commander of Draconian Realm Armed Forces, shimmered into being.

"And not a moment too soon, Kane," Draco started speaking without preliminary. "If you'd stayed in my chair two seconds longer I'd have flattened you right now the same way I'm going to flatten the Inner City by dawn tomorrow." The gross emperor burst forth with peals of wild, disgusting laughter. The sound echoed wildly through the spartan command bridge of the *Draconia* freezing the blood of every crewman and guardtrooper on duty.

Kane was the first to recover his composure. Draco may have been an effective ruler, but he did not gain the submission of his subjects by charming them to his side. Not by any means.

With an obsequious bow to the image of the Emperor Draco, Kane managed his customary well-oiled delivery of words. "We are honored by your majesty. Your decision to grant us the great pleasure of your presence flatters us beyond words."

"Sure it does, you scum!" Again the gross emperor burst into peals of rolling laughter, holding his flabby sides as if the sheer energy of his mirth would burst them open. "Now, what is the battle plan that you've worked out? And where is my sweet little pidgeon of a darling, the Princess Ardala?"

"Her highness, the Princess Ardala, has retired for the night, your Majesty."

"Really, now has she?" Draco's expression grew wary. "Kane, I find that rather strange."

"Strange, your Majesty?"

"Indeed." The gross image in the command chair leaned forward. "For one thing, Kane, I should think that Ardala would be most eager to observe the preparations for what must be the greatest planetary conquest in the history of space. To observe and to supervise, I should say."

"I have been delegated to oversee the preparations, your Majesty. The Princess Ardala resides her fullest confidence in my ability to command the preparations."

"Does she, now?" the emperor queried suspiciously.

"Why, yes, your Majesty," Kane said in his oiliest manner, bowing and scraping before the gross image in the command seat.

"The other reason for my discomfiture," the emperor continued, ignoring Kane's explanations as if they had never been spoken, "has to do with your own ambitions, Kane."

"My only ambition, your majesty, is to serve the Draconian realm to the best of my humble ability." Again, the swarthy-complexioned Kane bowed low before the immaterial image.

"Kane," Draco said with an impatient wave of one fat hand, "the only thing that befits you worse than your arrogant manner is your humble one. At least the first is sincere, obnoxious though it is. But when you try to act modest, you turn my imperial guts inside out."

"My greatest pleasure, your majesty," Kane bowed again.

"Oh, ho ho ho ho ho," Draco roared, "oh, ho ho ho!!! That's more like it. That's the boy, Kane. Now you listen to me." Once more he leaned forward, pointing an admonitory finger at the courtier.

"I know you've got your eye on the Princess Ardala, and I don't blame you. Even a father can spot a piece of choice woman flesh when he lays eyes on it, even if it is his own daughter. But you've got to prove yourself a worthy son-in-law for me, and a worthy consort for the future Empress of Draconia. You know, Kane, I have twenty-nine other daughters and twenty-nine sons-in-law, and never a worse conglomeration of weaklings, social-climbers and fops have ever disgraced a royal family tree.

"Ardala is my last, best hope for a posterity worthy of the name. That's why I've had my eye on you, sonny-boy!" He leaned back in the chair, scanning Kane appraisingly.

"I can handle the princess, my emperor, trust me for that," Kane said grimly.

"I doubt it, Kane. *I* could never do anything with her, and I'm her own father!" Draco gave another peal of laughter. "Well, let's see if your other efforts warrant keeping you alive, sonny-boy."

Kane swallowed visibly and beads of sweat appeared on his brow. "I—I think my efforts will speak for themselves, your Majesty. We are well within the earth's defense shield—the *Draconia* is at this very minute closer to the surface of Earth than any other ship of the realm has ever succeeded in getting, and that with the acquiescence of the earthers themselves."

"But what about your warcraft?" Draco demanded. "The flagship is useless without her armament—just a giant ocean-liner of the spacelanes unless her weapons are operational."

Kane smiled broadly. He knew, now, that he was on stronger ground than he had been in discussing the situation with regard to the Princess Ardala. He preened and approached the realistic image of the emperor. "All the warcraft are on board, your Majesty. All are in combat-ready condition, armed and prepared to strike in"—he checked the time by the command bridge's ship's chronometer—"exactly four hours. That will be at dawn, local time, below in the Inner City."

"Ahhhh!" Draco's exclamation was a long, drawn-out expression of pleasure, surprise and satisfaction. "That's very good, Kane, that's the kind of intelligence I like to receive. Well, I think you'll stay alive and out of the stoker gang for a while longer at least. I may even grant my daughter an interview and make note of some of your more attractive features in our discussion.

"Er—that reminds me—you *do* have some attractive features, Kane, do you not?"

The courtier smirked. "Your Majesty would know, of course. I would not deign to promote my own virtue in such a manner, it would hardly be seemly or modest, now would it, your majesty?"

"Hardly, Kane, hardly. But tell me something." The emperor had plucked a thread from his regal robe and was twiddling it, spinning it into a corkscrew one way, then the other, back and forth, over and over again.

"Anything your majesty wishes," Kane cooed.

"How is it that you tell me that our attack forces are aboard the *Draconia*, combat ready and all prepared to strike at the Inner City at dawn," Draco said.

"Yes, your majesty."

"While my intelligence sources within the Earth Directorate tell me that the Inner City Intercept Squadron boarded your starship only a few watches ago."

"Why, they did, your Majesty."

"They boarded you? How did that come about?"

"It was an obvious ruse, Draco. I let them think they had tricked us into letting them board, so they could surreptitiously check for armaments. They went away convinced that we carried none."

"You were hiding an attack fleet in your pockets, I suppose."

"We misled them successfully, Majesty. If I may respectfully suggest something to the emperor, full operational reports will be forthcoming in due course. Rather than dwell on what is already done, should we not direct our attention to what remains before us? In less than four hours we shall be attacking the Inner City and initiating the complete and final conquest of Earth!"

"You're right, Kane. Score one for the Killer, eh? All right, let me have the details of your plan. You're presently in orbit above the Inner City. In a few hours the sun will rise. Then—?"

"Then, my emperor. . . ." Kane moved away from the throne and its three-dimensional Person-Image. He picked up a pointer and began a formal briefing. The war-map he used was itself a projection, in three dimensions and full color, of the sector of space enclosed in a globular configuration centered upon the Earth and extending as far as the moon. The flagship *Draconia* showed in the map as a brilliant point of glowing white light.

The pointer which Kane held contained in its handle an array of microminiaturized control circuitry and a closed-beam transmitter controlled by Kane himself. Simply by manipulating the handle of the pointer he could alter the scale of the map, drawing back to present greater vistas or moving inward to magnify some section or feature of the map for closer examination. He could also change the center of the map, so that its focus radiated from the *Draconia*, the domed Inner City of earth, or any other point of his selection.

"At the first light of dawn, we launch our ships to attack all of earth's principal defenses, with particular attention, of course, directed to the Inner City. Our primary target will be the power source of the defense shield itself."

As Kane spoke he manipulated the controls in the pointer-handle, using the long silvery rod to direct Draco's attention—and that of everyone else on the command bridge of the *Draconia*—to particular features of the map.

Before Kane's pointer and Draco's approving eyes, the planned attack was simulated in miniature on the map. The focus became that of the *Draconia* as she hovered in orbit directly above the Inner City. The Earth below was bathed in darkness, save for the diamondlike, glittering lights of the Inner City.

The earth turned as always, but its rotation was

imperceptible from the *Draconia*—even the simulated *Draconia* of the star-map—because of the flagship's synchronous orbit.

Gradually a faint suggestion of rose coloration suffused the eastern horizon of the simulated earth. Simultaneously there appeared in the star-map a swarm of tiny lights, each as brilliant as that representing the *Draconia* but infinitely smaller. They hovered nearby for a brief interval. Then the map was bathed in a pure yellowish light as the corona and then the first arc of the photosphere of the sun appeared over the simulated horizon. The rays of the map-sun glittered on the dome of the Inner City, turning it into a dazzling vision of modernity, grace, and streamlined, efficient design.

Simultaneously the swarm of tiny lights dived earthward. Their formation was that of a delta-winged fighter, needle nose foremost. The delta-shaped formation swooped toward the domed Inner City. A simulation of earth's Starfighters swarmed upward to meet them, each craft of Colonel Deering's famous Intercept Squadron represented by a gleaming point of vermillion.

As the two fleets approached each other it became obvious that the diamondlike attackers vastly outnumbered the vermillion defenders. The Starfighters roared into their familiar fire-and-evade maneuvers but the diamond attackers matched them to the last degree, firing their own laser weapons until the vermillion defenders blossomed into orange and black puffs of smoke, then disappeared from the map.

When all of the Starfighters had been eliminated the diamond attackers turned their fire upon the Inner City itself, pouring laser flares into the shimmering dome until it literally melted away, leaving the Inner City a helpless hulk. Now the *Draconia* itself swung lower until, escorted by the glittering diamond attack-craft, it settled its massive bulk onto the main landing pad of the Inner City's central spaceport.

The Inner City was defeated.

Earth was conquered.

The Draconian Empire had added not merely another vassal-world to its holdings, but a wide-open gateway to the galaxies beyond. Vistas opened before Kane and Draco of new conquests, an infinite and unending string of conquests, stretching as far into the future as the imagination could foresee.

The crewmen, technicians, and guardsmen posted around the control bridge of the *Draconia* burst into spontaneous applause as Kane manipulated the handle of his pointer and the star-map with its projected war simulation faded back to a neutral gray.

Grinning ingratiatingly Kane bowed before the PersonImage of Draco seated on the throne. "Very pretty, Kane," the emperor said. "I hope that the actuality is as pleasant to participate in as your simulation was to observe."

Kane bowed before the image. "Such is my intention, your majesty. It has been calculated to the ninth decimal position. We cannot fail."

"Cannot fail, eh?" Draco rubbed his greasy chin. "Those famous last words have preceded many a disaster, Kane. For instance, I notice that you have our attack fleet approaching the Inner City *en masse*, then blasting their Starfighters out of the sky by virtue of superior numbers. But what if we have to thread a narrow attack corridor? We would then be prey to their anti-warship batteries."

"Believe me, your majesty, that has all been accounted for. I have followed the standard Draconian tactic of boring from within until the enemy's defensive strength is completely neutralized. Earth will hardly need to be conquered—it will fall into our hands like a rotten apple falling from its limb!" He matched his words with a two-handed gesture, holding his fleshy palms upward as if to catch a tumbling piece of fruit.

"For the sake of the realm, Kane, let us hope that you are right," Draco responded. "And also, I might add, for your own sake. If you have misled me as to the effectiveness of your plan, you'll yearn for the ease and comfort of the stoker gang long before I grant you the boon of final oblivion."

"Our plan will not fail, my Emperor."

"We shall see." Draco shifted back on his throne, placing his luxuriously shod feet on a footstool invisible to the occupants of the *Draconia*. "We shall see," Draco repeated. "In the meanwhile, please extend my congratulations to the Princess Ardala as soon as she arises. I wouldn't want her to miss the show this morning. My pretty little pidgeon-princess. Oh, ho ho ho ho ho ho!!!"

"I will deliver the imperial message," Kane bowed low.

With a sudden heave of his bulk, Draco rose to his feet, lifting his massive body from the throne where he had sat. For the moment his gross form and disgusting, self-indulgent mannerisms were gone. This man had not reached the absolute rule of the greatest empire the galaxy had ever known by being a fat and luxury-loving sybarite. That represented one side of his nature, true enough.

But within that flabby body there dwelled also a man of boundless energy, brilliant cunning, and unbendable will.

Suddenly that man stood before his throne, his PersonImage projected with holographic perfection to the control bridge of the *Draconia*. Suddenly that dominating, imperious figure raised one hand in the ancient symbol of conquest, the upright clenched fist.

Kane fell away from the PersonImage almost as if he had been struck a physical blow. The others scattered around the bridge gasped in surpise and awe.

"Valanzia!" the image of Draco roared, naming one of Draconia's great military triumphs.

"Valanzia!" the occupants of the bridge repeated, their voices rising in a crashing chorus that echoed off the sleek steel bulkheads of the flagship.

"Mortibundo!" the magnificent Emperor Draco roared.

"Mortibundo!" the crewmen and guardsmen repeated.

"And—Earth!" Draco shouted.

"Earth!" the others echoed. "Earth! Earth! Earth!"

As the word echoed and reechoed through the steel-walled control bridge of the *Draconia* the PersonImage of the emperor slowly faded into invisibility.

As soon as the emperor's form was fully gone, Kane pranced triumphantly back to the control chair whose image had been transformed into the imperial throne by Draco's holographic projection. The oily courtier threw himself into the chair, a triumphant grin spreading across his face.

"That, my fellow Draconians," he chortled, "is but a small indication of the favor which I hold with the Emperor Draco. And but a small sign of the authority I command in executing the invasion of Earth! Tomorrow at dawn I shall lead you to the beginnings of the greatest rise in the history of the empire. And you will all be with me!"

Like a mirror image of the absent Draco, Kane stood before the control chair, his clenched fist raised in the air. Like an echo of the emperor's words, he shouted "Valanzia! Mortibundo! Earth!"

The others echoed Kane.

"Dispatch the armament crews," he commanded. "Alert all warships for the attack! On my personal command—three—two—one—*execute!*"

With a final, ringing cheer, the Draconian warriors sprang to initiate the final and total conquest of unsuspecting Earth!

NINE

~~~~~~

An inconspicuous cargo hatch aboard the *Draconia* popped open. Two faces peered cautiously out into the corridor where young Draconian technicians, crewmen and troopers were pounding by, intent upon their assigned military tasks.

"This is no good, Twiki," the owner of one of the faces complained to the other. "There are soldiers everywhere. And we don't even know where to look for Captain Rogers."

The other of the pair squeaked his reply.

"Of course not, Twiki. I don't want to get caught either," Theopolis agreed. "But there's something terribly wrong here, I'm afraid. Those men are wearing battle gear. Helmets and armor. And carrying weapons. I thought the *Draconia* was an unarmed ship of commerce. We've got to find out what's going on. Come on, now, Twiki, come on."

In the royal stateroom of the Princess Ardala, Buck Rogers had crept from the barbarically furnished bed and stood silently looking down at its remaining occupant. The Princess Ardala slept soundly, her negligee still clinging to her in disarray. She was almost bathed in luxurious, exotic furs that she used for bed furnishings. A smile of blissful satisfaction was on her heavily sensual lips as she slept the sleep of one drugged by doctored Vinol.

Buck reached out with one hand and caressed her long, gleaming tresses. He breathed a sigh of fatalistic yearning, then drew back his hand and moved away from the bed, crossing the room to the door and stealthily drawing it open by the merest crack.

Outside the stateroom Buck saw Ardala's Tigerman bodyguard. The giant mutated creature stood faithfully on guard, his back to the door, his arms folded impassively. From his great throat there emerged a low rumbling sound that might have been composed half of a subliminal growl, half of a pleased, abstracted purr. Buck would never have wanted to face that guardian when Tigerman was alert for his attack. But Tigerman was guarding the stateroom now against intruders from outside—not protecting himself from attack within the stateroom!

Buck reached forward, cautiously lifted Tigerman's laser gun from its holster. Tigerman remained blissfully unaware of Buck's presence. The earthman examined the laser, set its dial for stun, raised it again and carefully squeezed the trigger. The giant bodyguard stiffened in his tracks, then toppled massively backward into Buck's waiting arms. Buck dragged the huge, still form into the darkened stateroom and tiptoed back into the corridor, drawing the stateroom door silently shut behind him.

Buck moved stealthily along the corridor, opened a well-marked hatch and descended a circular ramp. As he passed the levels of the *Draconia* he carefully observed the level designations marked on successive bulkheads in brilliant incandescent orange and black symbols. Beside each Draconian symbol was lettered the official designation of the flagship section located on that particular level of the ship.

With a jolt Buck halted before the designation he had been seeking. The symbol was a sinister one; the lettering said *Fightercraft Launch Deck, Magazine Section Red (1)*. Buck carefully slipped through the open hatchway onto the fighter launch deck, concealing himself in the shadows behind a pile of equipment crates. He peered out at the activity taking place on the deck.

The deck itself was chiefly in darkness, but a large number of overhead-mounted spotlights picked out a veritable beehive of busy activity.

Crewmen in varicolored jumpsuits, each suit keyed to its wearer's assigned duty, swarmed over a full squadron of fighters, preparing them for combat launch.

Carrier-carts loaded with laser weapons and explosive missiles trundled by Buck's hiding-place; the earthman was able to see every feature of the cart-driver's intent face. The driver might have seen Buck lurking in the shadows had he turned at the right moment, but he rolled intently by, thereby saving himself from the quick stun-blast that Buck was prepared to deliver to prevent premature discovery.

The ships themselves were arrayed in mathematically precise echelon-rows. The crewmen who swarmed around them wore Draconian gear, Draconian uniforms marked with Draconian insignia. Each battle-jacket bore a large reproduction of the familiar Draconian coat-of-arms stitched colorfully upon its back.

But the ships themselves were not Draconian!

With a gasp, Buck recognized the fightercraft being prepared in the Draconian flagship for combat duty. They were *pirate marauder ships!* The ancient emblem of piracy, a grinning white death's-head, was blazoned large on the snout of each of the pirate ships.

And the livid red and black stripes in which the fuselages were decked, gave the strange impression, here in the shadowy light of the launching deck, of an ancient symbol of death and destruction and sheer, malevolent evil, that Buck remembered learning about in his history classes back in the early 1980s.

They were formed like the evil, broken-limbed cross, the ancient swastika!

Suddenly Buck's attention was drawn away from the fighter craft by the approach of footsteps and the sound of voices engaged in low conversation broken by the nervous laughter of fighting men preparing to go into combat. Two helmeted Draconian troopers appeared near Buck. They were unaware of him, merely passing by the equipment crates behind which he was concealed. They stopped almost within arm's reach of Buck, exchanged a final few words, then separated.

One returned across the launch deck.

The other looked toward the hatchway, moved in that direction as if to mount the spiral staircase to another deck—but that was a mistake for him! Soundlessly, Buck leaped from his shadowy station, threw an arm around the throat of the trooper and dragged him in an instant back into the shadows. . . .

Things were moving quickly, now, toward a climax.

In another part of the *Draconia,* Kane, a grimly determined expression on his face, moved silently along one of the ship's main corridors. Crewmen whom he passed recoiled in fear. They knew Kane, and they knew that he was in no mood to be crossed.

And in still another area of the flagship a stranger pair of beings scuttered briskly along, one of them on his short, mechanical legs; the other, hanging from the neck of the first. The two of them reached a key intersection of corridors just as the impressive form of Kane, his face showing his deep concentration on his own thoughts, entered the intersection from the other corridor.

Twiki and Theopolis ducked back into an access way, barely in time to avoid a collision with one of Kane's heavily booted feet. "Look at that!" Theopolis exclaimed in a low voice. "Kane himself! *Brrr!*" His lights flashed faster than usual. "You mark my words, Twiki," the computer-brain went on, "if anything improper is going on aboard this ship, that traitor to everything decent is at the bottom of it. I don't like that Kane! I think we'd better follow him."

Twiki squealed.

"Of course you're frightened," Theopolis replied. "Who wouldn't be? But—we must follow Kane. It's our duty!"

Twiki revolved one hundred eighty degrees and scuttled off as fast as he could go, completely in the opposite direction Kane had taken.

"Twiki," Theopolis murmured furiously, "if the Draconians don't get us, and we make it back to Earth, I'm going to report you as an even bigger traitor than Kane. Do you know what they do to drones who betray the Earth?"

Twiki stopped in his tracks, cocked his head to one side as if deep in thought. After several seconds of utter silence he squeaked loudly, whirled around one hundred eighty degrees and scuttled off after Kane.

"I knew it," Theopolis said smugly. "I knew that once you'd given due consideration to duty and morality, Twiki, that your innate sense of patriotic obligation would prevail."

Behind the equipment crate where he had dragged the unconscious body of the Draconian trooper, Buck stripped his clothing off and donned that of the helpless man. He adjusted the trooper's helmet, fitting it carefully over his own head, then drew its curved polarizing filter-shield down over his face. Indistinguishable now from any of the Draconian troops moving among the deck crew of the flagship, Buck stepped out briskly onto the flight deck with its frantic but purposeful activity still in progress.

On the spiral ramp from which Buck had emerged onto the deck, the diminutive metal form of Twiki clattered downward, Theopolis attached to his neck. The drone halted in the shadowy portal and watched the activity on the deck. The two mechanical beings had arrived just in time to see Buck pulling his Draconian helmet on and adjusting its facemask. He was thus unknown to any of the personnel on the *Draconia*'s launching deck—

but he had been recognized by Theopolis and Twiki.

The drone squeaked in distress.

"I know," Theopolis answered in a low tone. "I know, Twiki, and I can hardly believe it myself." The computer-brain gave a despondent low groan. "I wish I could deny it but I can't, it was definitely Buck and he's wearing the uniform of our enemy."

Twiki squeaked.

"I don't care how valuable our people think the treaty between Earth and Draconia is, Twiki. Those are warcraft out there on that deck. That means that the treaty is a cruel hoax."

Twiki squeaked.

"Yes, I'm afraid we're finished, Twiki. I don't see how we can do our duty and still get out of here alive. But we can still perform one last service for our country, Twiki, for the people who created us." The flashing lights that made Theopolis's computer-face blazed into an expression of anger and determination. "We can still deal with Captain Rogers!"

Only a few dozen yards from Theopolis and Twiki, a crew of armaments technicians were busily withdrawing heavy laser torpedoes from ordnance lockers and placing them on dollies to be transported to waiting pirate marauder craft. Each dolly had the following information stencilled on it in glowing, incandescent words. *Warning, Live Ammo.*

Disguised in his Draconian trooper's uniform

and helmet, Buck Rogers strode up to the crew and joined in their efforts. They had brought an ammuition cart up to the front of one of the swastika-shaped fighter craft and were loading laser torpedoes into the forward firing tubes of the fighter. While the crewmen loaded torpedoes, Buck unobtrusively made his way to the rear of the fighter they were working on.

He hefted one of the heavy torpedoes overhead and muscled it into position in the focus-spot of the afterburner, secured it in place with a molybdenum bracket-winch and tested it with the weight of his body. No question remained—the ravening force of the torpedo was pent up, ready to be released at the crucial moment—but not at all in the way that the treacherous Draconian war-plan foresaw!

His face hidden behind its tinted plexiglass helmet-shield, Buck quick-marched from the tail of the marauder to the ammo cart and lifted another torpedo from it. On his way to the tail area of the next marauder fighter, he passed a Draconian guard corporal. The corporal, standing stiffly at parade rest, nodded to Buck as Buck passed him. The earthman returned the nod and continued his work.

Twiki and Theopolis, in the meanwhile, were working their way carefully along the wall of the launching deck, keeping to the shadows as much as possible, avoiding the scrutiny of the Draconian guard-troops as well as ship's personnel and fighter crews. Theopolis was speaking to Twiki.

"It's even worse than we thought it was," the computer-brain mourned, "those are warships of some peculiar sort. I don't know exactly what their markings mean, but they're obviously up to no good purpose. And now they're loading weapons and ammunition onto them! They're going to bomb the Inner City, Twiki, that's what they're going to do!"

The drone squealed shrilly.

"No," Dr. Theopolis said, more mournfully than ever. "Buck is on the Draconians' side. I don't know whether he was loyal to Earth before, and has gone over to the other side for some reason—or whether he was a Draconian agent from the start, Twiki, and had us all fooled until now. Oh, and I don't know which solution is the more distressing. Not that it all really matters very much anyway.

"But that doesn't make any difference now, Twiki. Listen carefully." Dr. Theopolis dropped his voice until he was almost whispering to the drone. "I'm going to ask you to do the most dangerous thing you've ever done, Twiki. Now stop it and hold still and listen to me, you can't run away from this! This is for our country and our planet, Twiki. There, now that's better...."

Kane, meanwhile, had been the object of Twiki's and Dr. Theopolis's surveillance, but the wily Kane, without even realizing he was being followed, pursued his habitual devious pattern of conduct and accidentally rid himself of his two unwanted followers.

He moved, now, through the corridor that brought him to the royal stateroom of the Princess Ardala. Outside the princess's door he found a Draconian guard-trooper standing at rigid and attentive attention.

"Guard," Kane snarled, "where is the princess's bodyguard, Tigerman?"

"I don't know, sir," the guard-trooper replied.

"How long have you been at this post?" demanded Kane.

"Only a few minutes, sir. I was out in the enlisted men's lounge, sir, off duty. Then I was told to report here for a temporary special assignment. Only the princess herself has the authority to relieve me from my post. And it is most important, sir. As you know, the princess is the only person aboard ship with the full authority to order the final assault on Earth."

"And you have not seen Tigerman?"

"Not all day, sir."

"That's very odd, soldier," Kane said accusingly. "You know the princess relies on Tigerman to protect her very life. She told you to guard her door?"

"No, sir. I haven't seen the princess either. A guardsman corporal brought me the message in the E.M.'s lounge. I didn't feel that it was my place to disturb the princess's privacy, sir."

"No," Kane agreed for once, "it wasn't your place. It's *mine!* Something very queer is going on aboard the *Draconia*. Soldier, if you want to stay out of the stoker gang, you remain here on duty come hell or high water! Let no one enter this room—or leave it! Not even Princess Ardala herself! You're under my personal command, and I'll personally see to your reward if you do a good job—or I'll nail your hide to the bulkhead and feed your insides to a nest of Algolian bookreviewer worms if you don't!"

"Yes, sir, Mr. Kane!" The soldier snapped to attention more rigidly than ever as Kane strode angrily away.

Back on the fighter-launching deck, Buck went about his strange business of bolting laser torpedoes into afterburners while the Draconian guardsman who had nodded to him went about his own business of patrolling the area. The work of the mechanics and technicians filled the launching deck with a constant clatter and din, so loud and so steady that the sound of a drone's mechanical scuttering went unnoticed.

Twiki lifted one deft mechanical hand toward the holster of the guard and carefully removed the laser pistol from its place. With the precious gun in his possession, Twiki scuttered away from the guard again. "Good work," Dr. Theopolis said softly to the drone. "We may have to sacrifice our own lives to do it, Twiki, but I think we may yet thwart this treacherous betrayal of all that we hold dear."

He paused, Twiki squeaked, then Theopolis said, "Oh, it's your life that you do hold dear. Well, my fine little quad, nobody lives forever. Think of it as a sacrifice made in a good cause. Oh, you want *me* to think of it that way, while you leave. Oh. Well, I'm sorry, that just cannot be arranged."

While the two mechanicals conversed, Buck finished setting up laser torpedoes in the last of the fighter craft's tailpipes. He turned to see Twiki and Theopolis standing directly before him. The quad held a Draconian guardsman's laser pistol in his hand and was pointing it directly at Buck's chest.

"Don't move, Captain Rogers," Theopolis commanded.

Buck froze.

"This isn't going to be pleasant for any of us," Theopolis went on. "We saw you before you pulled that mask over your face, so we know who you are. Now don't make us shoot you, Rogers. This weapon is *not* set to stun—do you understand me?"

Without answering the question, Buck gaped at the mechanicals. "Theopolis? Twiki? What are you guys doing *here*? Get away from this area. It's dangerous for you. And I've still got work to do here!"

"That we can see, Buck Rogers. You traitor!"

"Traitor!" Buck exclaimed. "Traitor! Oh! Can't you see what's happening, Theopolis?"

"I can," Theopolis's lights flashed angrily. "I'd say that someone was getting ready to bomb the earth—and that that somebody included Captain Buck Rogers on their team!"

"Don't you recognize the ships?" Buck asked.

"I don't see as that makes very much difference," Theopolis said coldly, "although I'll admit that they look a little familiar to me."

"It makes a great deal of difference," Buck insisted. "Look at them!" He pointed to the death's head insignia on the nearest marauder. "They're pirate ships!"

"Pirate ships?" Theopolis echoed, astounded. "Why in the cosmos should there be pirate ships aboard the Draconian flagship? I'm sorry, Captain, you'll have to do better than that. Now if you don't mind, we'll just escort you from this area—"

"No," Buck interjected. "You go ahead and shoot me if you must, Dr. Theopolis. But I warn you, if you do, it spells the sure doom of earth."

"Oh, come now, Rogers. I suppose you're going to tell me that those bombs you're loading onto the ships here are full of flowers and candy to drop on the pretty girls and the little children of the Inner City."

"Look," Buck lashed out verbally, "you half-baked load of electronic gibberish, I don't know what you think is going on. I can't expect you to know everything, of course, but have you ever heard of loading bombs in the *tailpipes* of a rocket ship?"

Twiki squeaked excitedly.

"You be quiet, Twiki," Theopolis scolded. "I'm getting confused enough by Buck, without your helping do it too."

"Well, maybe this will unconfuse you," Buck said angrily. "There are no pirate ships. There never were!"

"What?"

"That's right! They're Draconian bombers, and have been all along. Piloted by Draconian crews. They've been specially marked to make us think they were from some mysterious nest of raiders when they were from Draconia all along, working for the specific purpose of maneuvering Earth's leaders into a treaty with Draconia!"

Twiki squeaked.

"Then—but—if—oh—!" Theopolis's lights flashed in a pattern of confusion and disarray. After an astonishing display of lucent disharmony, the computer-brain finally got his circuits back into proper order. "But if it's a good treaty we'd have signed anyway. Why all the effort, the cost in lives and spacecraft?"

"Because it isn't a good treaty, as Earth would have realized if the false pirates hadn't panicked the Council into signing! The Draconian Empire was stymied by Earth's defensive shield and the Intercept Squadron, and the treaty is designed to get the imperial fleet past the shield and squadron safely—as it is in the process of getting them right now!"

"Of course!" Theopolis exclaimed, dazed. "Of course! Oh, Buck, what fools we've been!"

At that moment Kane stormed through the portal onto the launching deck. His jaw set in grim and angry determination, he headed straight for Buck and the others.

"You've got about ten seconds, Doc, to make up your mind," Buck said. "Do you want to believe Kane? Or me?"

"Some choice," Theopolis said.

"What about yourself," Buck went on. "Didn't your own logic circuits tell you I was on the level? What kind of computer do you call yourself, anyway?"

"As a matter of fact, Buck Rogers, my circuits are of the latest and most reliable design. And I must say, I think you're getting awfully damned personal questioning me like this." Theopolis's lights flashed angrily. "But as a simple truth, yes, my circuits did tell me to trust you."

"Then unless you want to consider yourself a box of spare parts for the Draconians' bridge engineers, you'd better go along with your original instincts."

Kane stopped, addressed a couple of soldiers nearby, then raised his eyes and scanned the launching deck carefully.

"All right," Theopolis said desperately. "But I'll

only trust you on the condition that you help us get to a communicator so we can warn the Inner City of this treachery."

"You'll have to take care of that, old robot chum," Buck said. "Because, on the chance that you don't get through, I'm going to have to make sure that none of these ships are able to launch!"

Theopolis's eyes flashed with alarm. What he saw was Kane running toward the spiral ramp, a guard at his side shouting and pointing with excitement. At the foot of the ramp Kane saw two more guards crouching over the body of an unconscious trooper who lay trussed up with his own underwear, his outer clothing taken!

"Out of time," Buck rasped at Theopolis. "They just found the guard I wiped out awhile ago."

Twiki squeaked frantically.

"All right," Theopolis said. "I'm convinced. We'll do our part. Good luck, Buck Rogers. I never doubted you for a minute, you know. Take the weapon—it won't do us any good, you're the one with the metabolism subject to forceful interruption!"

"None of us are going to make it out of this alive," Buck answered. "But there are millions of people down there who will, if we do our jobs. Now get going!"

Twiki squeaked, spun rapidly in a half-circle, and scuttered away, his metal feet scrabbling so fast across the metal deck that sparks struck up at every step he took.

Buck looked after the scuttering robots for a few seconds, then shifted his attention back to the job at hand.

Kane, meanwhile, had miraculously managed to miss seeing the earthman and his robot allies. He rose from a quick inspection of the trussed-up and unconscious guardsman, turned and stormed furiously up the ramp to the higher decks.

Buck Rogers, relieved at the departure of the courtier, resumed his work of technological sabotage of the Draconian raiders that were disguised as pirate marauder ships.

Kane charged up the corridor to the Princess Ardala's stateroom. He pounded up to the door, ordered the guardsman standing there aside.

"But sir," the young soldier protested, "my orders, sir—"

Kane shoved the trooper ruthlessly aside and slammed his hamlike fist again and again against the clanging metal of the door. "Ardala!" Kane shouted. "Get up! Open the door!"

Inside the stateroom Ardala's eyelids fluttered open at the racket. She felt in the furs beside her, murmuring in a half-sleeping voice, "Oh, Buck, was I dreaming, or—Buck? Buck, where did you—Buck!"

She sat up, alarmed, then fell back happily on the bed. "Oh, there you are, my darling!" She leaned over and started to press her face against the back of the head of the other occupant of the bed. Instead of ordinary hair she felt her cheek brush coarse, bristly fur.

She leaped back in alarm and screamed as the other rolled over to reveal slitted eyes, the fur-covered countenance, the pointed ears and the terrible fangs of—Tigerman!

Outside the princess's stateroom the screaming from inside echoed frighteningly off steel bulk-heads, sending the hair crawling on the neck of Kane. It wasn't that Kane was so incredibly fond of the princess. She certainly was an appealing bundle of charms, but Kane knew that women's bodies were readily available to men in positions like his own. As an old Earth politician had once commented in a moment of uncharacteristic candor, power is an aphrodisiac.

But Ardala was Kane's means of access to the throne of Draconia! Without Ardala, Kane was just one more power-hungry climber, essentially no different from a brigade of other politicians, bureaucrats and military leaders. His leadership of the Earth-conquering expedition was a major point in his favor at Draco's court, and for all the emperor's expressed scorn during his recent Person-Image appearance, Kane knew that he had scored high in the conqueror's estimation.

But there were thirty princesses of the realm, each of them ambitious to sit upon the throne of empire once Draco had gone to join Caesar and Genghis Khan, Napoleon and Attila the Hun,

Adolf Hitler and Charlemagne and Stalin and all the other shades of the legendary conquerors of history. And twenty-nine of those princesses, jealous of her prospective power, had chosen for her prospective prince consort a weakling whom she could manipulate to suit her whim.

In the short run it made for smooth sailing in the households of the twenty-nine princesses and their wimplike husbands. But in the long run it left the Emperor Draco with no suitable heir and with the prospect of a dynasty that would collapse into rubble almost the instant his own strong hand was gone from the helm.

Only Ardala still had the promise of providing Draco with a son-in-law worthy to sit on the throne beside herself once Draco was gone. And only Ardala's choice of a mate held the promise, to Draco, of his living to see a grandchild worthy of continuing his dynasty down through the ages.

Kane saw himself as Ardala's husband, the thirtieth and sole worthy son-in-law of the Emperor Draco, the prospective prince consort of the Draconian Realm, and ultimately, through his wife once she became empress, the *de facto* tyrant of the greatest array of worlds ever brought beneath the sway of a single ruler.

If anything happened to Ardala—anything to prevent Kane from marrying her and becoming prince consort—his plans were dashed. The crown would descend to one of the other princesses, one of the other sons-in-law would become prince consort, and Kane's whole elaborate projection would lie in wreckage.

And now—scream after pealing scream came from the stateroom of the Princess Ardala. Kane didn't bother to send for the ship's locksmith to open the resisting stateroom door. One futile blow from his jackbooted heel made the door shudder but failed to spring the lock. Kane waited no longer to draw his laser pistol, adjust its beam to minimum diameter and maximum intensity, and blast open the heavy-duty lock.

Another vicious kick from Kane's heavy boot and the door flew open, crashing back against the bulkhead inside the stateroom and sending a decorative coat-of-arms tumbling noisily to the floor. Kane and the guard-trooper pounded into the room, halting in shock at the sight that they beheld.

The Princess Ardala was sitting bolt upright in her fur-covered bed. Her negligee was pulled halfway over her head, her long hair hung in disarray around her face and she was screaming at the top of her lungs.

Beside her in the bed, frantically struggling to escape the entangling folds of satin sheets and thick fur comforters was the princess's usual bodyguard, Tigerman. His catlike face held an expression of confusion and alarm, and his throat was giving forth a series of sounds that' neither Kane nor the soldier had ever heard before, sounds that sounded like a combination whimper of fear and howl of despair and confusion.

"What—" Kane exclaimed as he tried desperately to assimilate the unprecedented scene before him. The Princess Ardala was not known in the Draconian Realm for extreme social fastidiousness, but bedding down with Tigerman was something beyond even the reach of Draconia's court gossip.

"What's going on?" Kane managed on the second attempt. Then, as he got a better grip on himself, he demanded angrily, "Your highness—are you out of your mind? What of the legitimacy of the royal line?"

"Take him away!" Ardala screamed. "How dare you suggest that I—that we—that a princess royal of Draconia would ever—!"

"The facts, Ardala—" Kane shouted excitedly.

"Execute that—that—animal!" Ardala ordered the guardsman. "Do it right here and now! Use your laser pistol!"

"No," Kane ordered the soldier coolly. "Place him under arrest and hold him in solitary confinement until I can question him."

"What!" Ardala shrieked. "Kane, you countermand my order?"

"Under the circumstances, princess, yes, I do!"

Tigerman, finally free of the entangling bedclothes, growled angrily and lunged toward Kane.

Kane raised his laser pistol and sent a single bolt of pure energy surging across the narrow space that divided him from the mutated animal. The courtier stepped coolly aside as Tigerman, stunned and paralyzed by the force of the laser beam, clattered to the floor inches from the man's heavy, polished boots. With a laugh and a sneer, Kane spurned Tigerman with the toe of one boot, turning the heavy body over onto its back.

"Drag this animal away," Kane instructed the guard-trooper. "Put him in irons. Let him communicate with no one, and don't bother to exert too much effort on his happiness or comfort. I'll issue further instructions later, as to what to do to expunge the stain he has placed on the royal escutcheon of the House of Draco!"

The guard saluted and stepped into the corridor to summon several more uniformed troopers. They dragged the body of the still helpless Tigerman away, and Kane slammed the stateroom door shut behind them.

"Well, well, well," Kane's words almost oozed from his mouth once he and Ardala were alone, "so the little princess has taken to playing with pussycats in the royal bedroom. Or should I say, only tomcats need apply?"

"You've some explaining to do, Kane!" the princess snapped angrily.

"*I* have?" Kane echoed incredulously. "*I* have explaining to do? You are the one with the peculiar taste in bed partners, my princess. Besides, I've been busy tending to the business of his majesty, the Emperor Draco. And I can tell you that his majesty will be less than delighted when he hears of the goings-on aboard the royal flagship.

"Aside from your highness's eccentric little love exploits, there's been a traitor planted aboard this ship. Two of my guards have been assaulted, and with all due respect to your highness," and Kane made a mocking, exaggerated bow, "I am frankly more concerned over the presence of a saboteur than over your highness's odd sexual appetite."

"Traitor? Saboteur? What would I know of that?" Ardala demanded.

"I suppose nothing, Ardala. You've obviously been otherwise occupied."

"I'll deal with your insolence later, Kane. This little scene has not at all the meaning that your filthy little mind assigns to it. I was somehow tricked. Drugged, probably. I passed out in my bed, and when I awoke it was to find Tigerman beside me, apparently as puzzled and distressed by the whole matter as I was."

"A very convincing tale," Kane cooed. "Of course, her highness's word is above reproach, just like the virtue of Caesar's wife. Hah!"

"Meanwhile," Ardala commanded Kane, "you will give the order to launch our attack on Earth. At once!"

"I think not," Kane countered. "We can't attack until your father's forces arrive to support us."

"Oh, Kane, you're as much of a spineless weakling as any of my twenty-nine sisters' weakling husbands. Of course we don't need my father. We have overwhelming strength even without him, we have the element of surprise, and we have our own influence boring from within the Inner City to weaken their defenses."

"It's too dangerous," Kane shook his head, "too risky. Let's wait for the emperor."

"You gutless fool," Ardala scorned him. "Do you want to be the conqueror of Earth—or do you want to be an underling in the army of the conqueror? If we go ahead, you and I can be sitting together on the throne of Earth by the time Draco heaves his fat carcass into view. *We* can be, you and I, Kane.

"But if you don't have the nerve to come along in the attack, why, I'll go ahead and do it myself. And sit alone on the throne of a conquered world!"

Pacing back and forth on the richly furred floor of Ardala's chamber, Kane frowned in concentration. The strain he was under was obvious. His forehead burst into sweat. His hands trembled and he clenched his fists to make them stop.

"All right!" he exclaimed. "All right, Ardala! I concede your point. We will attack."

"At once," she pressed him.

"Yes, very well. At once."

"A good decision, Kane." She rose to her imposing height, the exposure of her body as ignored as if she were clad in full military array instead of a filmy wisp of negligee. "Now, get out of here and go issue your commands. I wish to be alone while I dress."

TEN

~~~~~~

The communications bridge of the *Draconia* was bathed at all times in an overwhelming, gloomy murk. The darkness was no accident of poor starship design or construction. It was a deliberate and planned aspect of the starship's architecture, for in this room the dim red lights of dials and the green and yellow tracers of 'scope surfaces were monitored constantly by some of the most highly trained communications engineers and technicians of the Draconian realm.

They needed the darkness to give maximum visibility to their screens and dials and dimly flashing lights, and their skill was so highly prized by the Draconian officer corps that they were required to undergo a special hour-long period of accustomization to the darkness before the beginning of each of their shifts, and a similar period of reacclimatization to normal lighting at the end.

The room beeped and hummed and chattered to itself as messages came from every part of the giant ship and from every remote spacecraft and planet with which it was in contact, to be read out, translated, processed, stored, manipulated, retrieved, recoded, and retransmitted to its assigned destination.

Communications shifts were long, and in exchange for their sacrifices, commo crews were pampered by the ship's quartermaster. No other duty station received catered meals while at their assignments! The chief communications console operator sat with his eyes glued to a red tracer screen, muffled earphones clapped to the sides of his head. An empty food tray stood forgotten on top of his console, nearly full containers of condiments and spices resting among the emptied dishes of roast Betelgeusan swamp hen and iced Plorusian slug-jell.

The console operator's seat was located on one side of the big, desklike contrivance. The other side of the console was an area of simple darkness and no particular purpose except to provide access to service panels for maintenance work on the console when it was taken off-line.

From this darkness a small, metallic hand rose, felt silently and unnoticed among the condiments and spices on the meal-service tray, finally found the shaker of ground black pepper. A small, rounded, metallic head rose over the edge of the console. A pair of artificial optical sensing devices focussed on the console operator.

The hand swivelled on an electronically powered and computer-circuit-guided arc, lifted the pepper shaker and sent a small cloud of pepper-grounds, invisible in the murkily lit communications room, floating toward the operator. The metallic hand silently placed the pepper shaker back on the meal-service tray. The head and the hand both disappeared back into the shadows on the service-area side of the communications console.

The operator's concentration on his screens and the hums and carrier tones in his earphones was interrupted. He found his eyes beginning to itch, then to burn and water. The images of the screens and tracer beams before him swam and wobbled through the tears. His nose began to itch, too, and a terrific sneeze drowned out the signals in his earphones. He sneezed again, then again.

He pulled off his headset, rubbed his burning eyes with smooth knuckles uncalloused by other than mental labor over the years. He scribbled a note on his log, jotting down the chronometer reading of the moment, as best he could make it out through his running tears, wrote next to it, in a disorganized scrawl, *Temporary relief, personal needs,* and his initials.

He headed for the nearest lavatory to get some running water and rinse the mysterious irritant from his eyes and nose.

As soon as the technician was out of range, Twiki scuttled around the end of the console and hopped up onto the operator's stool. At his height of three feet, the quad was as tall as the operator was when seated on the stool.

"Quick now, as we planned," the rich voice of Dr. Theopolis sounded. But it sounded in a tone little above a whisper so it was inaudible to the other technicians in the room over the hum and clicks and chatter of the scientific instruments, and just as Twiki and Theopolis, protected by the murk and gloom of the commo bridge, would be virtually invisible except to someone approaching close to the temporarily vacated console.

Twiki, using his astonishing deft and fast-moving mechanical hands, began setting switches and adjusting tuner-knobs on the console. Theopolis said again, in his low tone, "Good work, Twiki. Now set me down close to the microphone so I won't have to talk any louder than this."

The drone carefully removed Theopolis from around his neck and set the box of flashing lights down on the console's surface. He reached and adjusted a directional microphone so that it was as close to Theopolis as he could get it, and pointed directly at his voder-circuit.

"Earth Directorate Emergency Channel," Theopolis said into the microphone. His voice was pitched low but its tone was incredibly urgent. "Earth Directorate Emergency Channel. Top pri-

ority, Computer Council, Inner City—Rating
A-A-A-Zero-One. Urgent!"

A thousand miles below the flagship *Draconia*'s
synchronous orbit, the Earth Directorate Communications Center—by a cosmic irony, the virtual
duplicate of the commo bridge of the *Draconia*—
was also kept in 24-hour operation. Normal com-
mercial and administrative messages could wait
for regular business hours, but the emergency
channel was kept open at all times, and the technicians monitoring it were on duty in unbroken
rotating shifts.

The duty officer at the central communications
console picked up the covert transmission from the
Draconia and responded to it at once. "Computer
Counsellor Theopolis and Quad Twiki, you are
cleared for immediate transmission on emergency channel. Please proceed." Turning aside to
a smartly uniformed cadet-orderly, the duty officer
snapped, "Get on the low-frequency local console.
Shoot off a message to Colonel Deering and make
it fast!" The cadet leaped to comply with his instructions.

Even before Theopolis could initiate his message there was a beeping from the low-frequency
console and the cadet called to the duty officer,
"Colonel Deering on line, sir."

"Dr. Theopolis, Colonel Deering," the commo
officer said, "I'm patching you both through now

so you can exchange information via my console without delays. On line!"

He snapped a red toggle switch and the circuit hummed into life.

"This is Dr. Theopolis, ex-officio representative of the Council of Computers," the rich voice said softly.

"Yes, doctor," Wilma replied. "This is Colonel Deering. Where are you? How did you get on the emergency channel?"

"I'm on board the flagship *Draconia*. I followed Captain Rogers as you ordered, Colonel. Now hear this: the *Draconia* is not—repeat, *not* an unarmed vessel! She's filled with bombers and she's about to launch a full-scale attack on the Inner City!"

"But how—" Wilma gasped. "Where did they come from? I was there. I personally inspected the landing bay and found it empty!"

"There's no time to discuss it now, Colonel! You've got to scramble the Intercept Squadron— right now, at once!"

"Yes, doctor, of course you're right. Good luck to you!" Colonel Deering clicked off the patched transmission and punched buttons on her personal communicator control panel. As soon as the new commo linkage was established she spoke breathlessly into her minimike. "Dr. Huer—Permission to scramble fighter craft! I was right about Buck Rogers—that traitor! The Draconians are about to launch an attack!"

She was entirely right, as the scene aboard the *Draconia's* command bridge gave testimony. Kane was in full command, military chief of the ship under imperial authority from the Princess Ardala. From his command post he addressed the entire ship via electronic linkage. "Battle stations! Marauders prepare to launch! Stand by at my countdown. Five . . . four . . . three . . . two . . . *attack!*"

The tiger-striped marauder craft shot forward from the flagship, each menacing shape jolting into the vacuum as its catapult launcher delivered it the initial thrust that would start it into space with the velocity required to start its rocket engines. At one side of the *Draconia's* launching deck Buck Rogers, still arrayed in imperial uniform, smiled a grim, expectant smile.

In the *Draconia's* commo center Theopolis remained where Twiki had placed him. The console operator's earphones were now affixed incongruously to the audio pickup circuits of the computer-brain.

His lights flashing with grim urgency and dedication, Dr. Theopolis whispered to his quad associate, relaying messages as they arrived through his earphones. "War is declared, Twiki," Theopolis said huskily. The drone nodded solemnly, indicating that he understood the gravity of the situation.

In the deeps of space two forces of sleek fighting craft sped on collision course. One was the

Intercept Squadron, launched from Earth's Inner City and rocketing at top speed for the *Draconia* and its deadly parasites. The other was the lurid red and black striped pirate marauders launched by the *Draconia*'s catapults.

With imperial discipline the marauder pilots simultaneously clicked on their rocket-fuel feedlines and tapped their engine-starter controls.

In the command ship of the Intercept Squadron, Colonel Wilma Deering radioed her pilots. "This is Blue Flight Leader. Attack bombers as they launch. Then we'll go after the mother ship."

She received a startling reply from her forward observer pilot. "There are no fighters to attack, Leader. Take a look in your distance scope!"

"That doesn't make sense!" Wilma exclaimed. But she followed her eff-oh's recommendation and snapped on her distance scope, just in time to see the greatest fireworks display in the history of explosives.

In perfect unison and in perfect formation, the entire fleet of Draconian attack bombers disguised as pirate marauder craft, blossomed into a precision array of orange and black puff-balls, silently filling space with their vaporized metal while shooting off showers of white-hot fragments that were too massive and were blown away from the bombers too rapidly to have time to vaporize.

"They're dying of their own deceit," Wilma whispered. "I don't see how, but somehow their entire force of bombers has blown itself to smithereens! All right!" Suddenly she was no longer the wondering observer but the crisply effective military commander. "All Starfighters regroup," she spoke over her radio link, "form attack arrays and prepare to finish off the Draconian mother ship!"

The *Draconia*, gigantic though she was, had endured considerable damage from the force of the exploding marauders and the impact of a sizable number of heavy, high-velocity fragments that acted exactly like shrapnel when they impacted. The launching deck itself was the most heavily effected area. On it the forms of dead, wounded, or simply trapped Draconian personnel lay pinned in the wreckage of the catapults and service cranes.

One of the bodies was not that of a Draconian, although it wore Draconian garb. It was Buck Rogers. Buck moved a little, moaned once, then was still.

In the communications center, the console operator had failed to return to his station, sidetracked by the violence and surprise of the destruction of Draco's pirate marauder squadron. Instead of the regular operator, Twiki and Theopolis continued to man the console. Theopolis was saying to the drone, "Did you hear Wilma, Twiki? She'll kill Captain Rogers. We've got to stop her! Come in, Colonel Deering, come in!"

He heard the pop of her line opening to receive

his call. "You can't attack, Colonel," Theopolis pleaded. "You'll kill Captain Rogers!"

"That would be no great loss, doctor!" Wilma swung her Starfighter into a surging, swooping bank. The remainder of her Intercept Squadron maintaining careful formation, Wilma swept into a devastating laser run against the great, lumbering hulk of the *Draconia*.

Aboard the giant starship Princess Ardala of the Draconian Realm stood before the portal of her stateroom, gaping in shock at the ravening fury of the explosions outside as her fleet of attack bombers, painted in their pirate ship disguises, were utterly destroyed. The door of the stateroom swung open before the furiously booted kick of Kane.

"This is your doing, Ardala!" Kane snarled angrily. "I ought to leave you on the *Draconia* to be blown up by those cursed Starfighters, but I'm going to keep you alive and drag you before your father so he'll know who is responsible for this disaster! I have an emergency escape pod ready to launch. It can carry us far enough for your father's ships to find us."

"Never!" the princess gasped, white-faced with shock.

"Oh, no! You're not going to escape your medicine! For once I'm going to enjoy this," Kane growled. In long, eager strides he crossed the room and smashed the princess across the face with his fat, open-palmed hand. She staggered beneath the force of the brutal attack. He grabbed her by her long, glossy tresses and dragged her, shrieking in helpless fury, from the room.

Meanwhile the attack on the *Draconia* was proceeding with all the unleashed deadliness of the Intercept Squadron's Starfighters. Buck Rogers had recovered consciousness and struggled from beneath the rubble on the launch deck. Realizing that the *Draconia* was doomed, he began to run, searching frantically for Twiki and Dr. Theopolis.

An ammunition storage bunker on the flight deck exploded into a thunderous cloud of smoke and flame. Buck was knocked flat, again unconscious. Flight deck technicians scattered frantically; a damage control officer clicked into the ship's loudspeaker system and cried, "Clear flight deck immediately! Burning bunker fire threatens to spread to main ship's magazine!"

Klaxons blared, sirens screamed, the few surviving Draconians fled frantically up and down the circular ramp, hoping to get away from the main ammo dump before it went up.

Kane entered the main command bridge of the *Draconia*, still dragging the Princess Ardala, by now limp and almost unconscious, behind him. Kane pulled himself together enough to demand a situation report from the duty officer of the bridge.

"I—I don't know what's happening, sir," the officer stammered. "Our ships—they launched perfectly—everything was going according to plan.

Then suddenly—all at once—I don't know what happened, sir. They all just—exploded. All of them!"

"That's impossible," Kane grumbled in the face of the evidence. "All right, we'll look into that later. Right now, we've got to fight with what we have left. Direct all batteries to engage those Starfighters in direct anti-spacecraft fire." Kane turned and headed for the command seat.

Before he could reach it a form materialized in the seat, the functional shape of the furniture transforming itself into an ornate imperial throne. The figure was that of the Emperor Draco, and he was already in mid-bellow and full, red-faced wrath when he appeared. "What in the name of the realm is going on?" he demanded. He raved and smashed his fists against the arms of the throne. "I'm still five thousand miles away and you've initiated the attack! I want to know why!"

Kane stood trembling before the emperor. "I—I—" he stammered. Then, in the midst of his confusion, an inspiration struck that might yet get him off the hook and shift the blame for the day's debacle onto another. "I was just following orders, your majesty," he purred in sudden self-composure.

"*You* were following orders, Kane?" The emperor roared. "*You?* I thought you were in charge of that ship. Top military administrator. Now, whose orders do you think you were following—the Earth Directorate's?"

"No, your worship. I was following the orders of the imperial crown representative on this ship, the Princess Ardala."

"The princess?" Draco bellowed. "And did she order you to have all of my ships disintegrate before they could even get into the battle? Do you know what a marauder costs, Kane?"

"Your Majesty, I—that is, sire—" Kane broke down, unable longer to face the wrath of Draco.

"I'll tell you something, Kane. Yes, Killer," Draco hissed, and somehow his hiss was more terrifying than his shout. "Yes, I know they call you Killer. Well, you're going to get a taste of your own medicine, Kane. If either you or the Princess Ardala survive this debacle, I want you before me, scourged and in chains, within twenty-four hours. Then we'll find out what fun really is!"

And, roaring with bitter, raging laughter, Draco faded slowly from the bridge of the flagship.

Wilma Deering's Intercept Squadron had settled by now into a steady pattern, circling the *Draconia*, blasting at the giant hulk that quivered, now, without resistance, then banking away, zeroing in, and making another pass at the *Draconia*. Wilma herself led the attack, and from the cockpit of her Starfighter she saw a trail of flaming debris streaming from the battered starship.

Then there was a sudden opening where none had been before, a black cavity in the side of the *Draconia*, a puff of launching material, and an emergency pod streaked away from the battered hulk of the spaceship. Two tiny figures, far too small for Colonel Deering to make out from her Starfighter, huddled in the pod, in mortal fear that they might never be picked up by the minions of Draco and in equal fear that they might be found by those very forces.

On the ruined launch deck of the starship Buck Rogers regained consciousness a second time. His uniform was shredded, his skin bruised and bloodied, every muscle in his body seemed to be in agony and every bone was bruised if not worse. But he was alive, aware, and mobile. He struggled to shove aside the wreckage that kept him from escaping the flight deck.

Wilma Deering turned back to the *Draconia;* the escape pod was too small, too fast, and too far gone to warrant pursuit. But the main target was still at hand.

"The ship's about ready to blow," a Starfighter pilot murmured through the intercom, reaching Wilma and all the others in their ships.

"Withdraw from combat area, all ships. I'm going in to try and find Twiki and Dr. Theopolis."

From the burning hulk a voice reached Wilma's radiophones. Even through the roaring and the electronic crackle of space, Dr. Theopolis's rich, mellow voice remained distinctive. "Forget us," Theopolis urged, "we're just machines anyhow. Try and find Buck!"

"Buck!" Wilma exclaimed. "After his treason to earth, let him die with his true friends, the Draconians!"

"Wilma, he was no traitor to earth!" Theopolis pleaded. "Buck was a double, a triple agent. He was the one who sabotaged the pirate marauders! He single-handedly won this battle for Earth! And he was the one who sent us to warn you, earlier!"

Wilma's face was anguished. "Theopolis—why didn't you tell me! I'm coming in onto the launch deck. Somehow I'll get in, I don't know how! But I'll make it. Get Twiki to bring you and meet me there." To the rest of her squadron Wilma directed, "Remain in parking orbits near *Draconia*. I'm going in to attempt a rescue operation!"

Twiki lifted Theopolis from the commo console and placed him around his neck. He scuttled for the circular ramp and headed at top speed from the communications bridge to the launch deck. He came scuttering off the ramp and onto the deck, maneuvering with astonishing skill through the heaps of smouldering rubble. As he passed each pile of wreckage he gave it a quick optical scan. Finally he found the pile that held Buck Rogers pinned.

"Buck!" Theopolis exclaimed from Twiki's chest. "Buck, old fellow, so pleased to find you alive and reasonably well."

"Never mind that," Buck shouted. "The magazine's going to blow any minute now!"

"Don't worry, Buck, help is on the way." Twiki

halted in his tracks and began peeling girders and plates away from the place where Buck was trapped.

From his side, Buck pitched in, too, heaving and hauling at wreckage to get it out of the way. "What do you mean," he gasped between exertions, "what help is on the way?"

"Wilma's going to bring her Starfighter in here and take us all out of here."

"But she can't!" Buck exclaimed. "Look at this deck! She'll never land safely. She'll be killed."

There was a low rumble and the entire hulk of the *Draconia* lurched and trembled.

"It's going now!" Buck shouted.

Twiki clamped his metal hands on the last girder prisoning Buck and hurled it aside with his superhuman strength. Little clouds of smoke curled from beneath his shell at the exertion he had made, but—Buck Rogers was free!

The three of them began to run at top speed through the smoke.

Wilma Deering brought her sleek Starfighter to the *Draconia*, jockeying it through alleyways and openings hardly wider than its metal wingspan. There was only one way that that miraculous landing could have been made. No computer-controlled ship could have done it, no preprogrammed procedure could have brought the Starfighter to its perilous berth aboard *Draconia*. The only way it could have been done was the way it had been done: Wilma Deering had switched off her Auto-

Flite computer and piloted the Starfighter to its landing, flying, to use an old aviator's expression, by the seat of her pants.

The instant that the craft ground to a halt, Wilma had thrown open its hatch and was calling to the others. "Twiki! Theopolis!"

The little drone scuttered to the side of the Starfighter and scrambled to safety inside the cockpit.

Buck Rogers stood beside the craft, looking straight into Wilma Deering's eyes. Neither of them spoke for a long moment, then Wilma, with a sob, blurted, "Buck, I was wrong. I was all wrong about you."

"Who's complaining," Rogers answered. "We can talk about it later." He put one hand on the Starfighter's wing and vaulted into the spacecraft behind its beautiful pilot.

"Hang on!" Wilma urged. She gunned the engine and the Starfighter surged from the launch deck of the giant hulk. The fighter craft zoomed away from the *Draconia*, accelerating as it moved. Suddenly the sky behind the Starfighter was filled with a flash of terrible light, and a shockwave crashed into the Starfighter, sending it tumbling through space before Wilma could manage to regain control and stabilize the orbit of the craft.

Over one shoulder she could see the *Draconia*. Like a single huge bomb the size of a middle-sized city it was erupting in a chain reaction of smoke and flame and flashes of explosives. Before

Wilma's very eyes—and those of all the pilots of the Intercept Squadron as well as Buck, Theopolis and Twiki—the *Draconia* disintegrated into a mass of hot, smouldering rubble.

"There goes the Trojan horse of space," Buck Rogers muttered.

"This is Blue Leader," Wilma snapped across the radio communicator. "Target utterly destroyed. Intercept Squadron, return to Earth base at once."

Buck slid his arm gently around Wilma's shoulders, feeling for the moment like a teenage boy headed home from a date with his favorite sweetheart.

Wilma smiled, pressed her cheek for a moment against Buck Rogers' shoulder, then sat upright again and concentrated on swinging her Starfighter back into its place at the point of the squadron.

The formation of sleek spacecraft arrowed downward to the Earth, headed for a heroes' welcome by Dr. Huer and the rest of the Earth Directorate.

EPILOGUE

~~~~~~

The festivities had ended, the celebration was over. Earth returned to the business at hand: the rebuilding of its wrecked civilization, the restoration of its ruined ecology, the reclamation of lands and seas poisoned by centuries of greedy exploitation and decades of deadly war.

Within the Inner City the Council of Computers was meeting in full, formal session within the Palace of Mirrors. The Draconian throne had been removed from its place on the dais of honor and broken up for firewood and silver and gold and precious gems. In its place there was a circle of benches, each bearing a crimson pillow, each pillow bearing the shiny-surfaced box of a computer-brain, each brain ceremoniously flashing its array of colored lights.

Buck, Wilma, and Dr. Huer clustered on the scroll-bench, while the glistening hall was virtually filled with diplomats and ordinary citizens wearing their most splendid outfits. The drone Twiki, his bearings replaced and gaskets refurbished after the astounding—and nearly suicidal—exertion of saving Buck Rogers, trotted ceremoniously up to Dr. Huer. As usual, the quad was carrying Dr. Theopolis carefully around his neck.

"Dr. Theopolis will state the charges," Huer intoned ceremoniously.

"When we were in the communications center aboard the *Draconia*," Theopolis intoned smoothly, "we discovered a direct tie-line. It ran from the Draconian command post to a direct radio-link to the traitor who was smuggling out our secret Starfighter evasion tactic tapes to the pirates. The pirates whom we now realize were actually the Draconians themselves!

"This traitor was also highly instrumental in pushing through the infamous false treaty with Draconia, that came within a hair's breadth of costing earth her precious freedom and delivering her into Draconian vassalage under the iron heel of Kane and the Princess Ardala."

Dr. Huer considered the terrible charges long and seriously. At last he asked, "Is the traitor present in this assembly?"

Theopolis said, "He is, sir."

"Please point him out, Dr. Theopolis," Huer requested.

Moving with ceremonial deliberation—and perhaps still feeling the after-effects of his near destruction aboard the dying enemy starship—Twiki crossed to the ring of cushioned computer-brains.

"Members of the Council," Theopolis intoned solemnly, "I am saddened to say, it was one of our own kind. Yes, one of us who have been entrusted with the wellbeing of the Inner City and all of earth and her peoples. A computer was programmed by the treacherous Kane before he defected from Earth to serve the Princess Ardala and the Draconian Realm.

"One of us, my colleagues, was programmed to appear normal—but to oppose our true best interests and to give away our most vital secrets."

Twiki raised a gleaming metallic arm and pointed at one of the computer brains.

"The traitor," Theopolis announced solemnly, "is none other than my own dear colleague, Dr. Apol."

A gasp went up throughout the hall.

When order was restored, Dr. Huer intoned ceremoniously, "The Council will pronounce sentence upon the traitor."

Drone-pages resembling Twiki advanced from behind each of the computer-brains and turned their cushions so they were all facing toward the guilty Dr. Apol.

"Now, let's not be hasty," Apol stammered. "I had no choice in this, you know. My actions were imposed on me. That nasty Kane twisted my circuits so that I thought I was doing right when I was doing wrong. He corrupted my wiring, altered my perceptions, decoded my programming, falsified my memory bank."

His voice slowed down as the other computers glared at him. Their flashing lights seemed to radiate a force that was slowly sapping Apol's energy and his will to continue.

"Comrades," Apol resumed, "I am one of you. I am a fellow computer. What do we care about these puny humans? Let them have their treaties and their wars. We are the heirs of intelligence."

The others increased the intensity of their radiations. Apol's voice slowed, slurred, faltered. "Fellow computers. Brothers. Have mercy on your own kind. Your own kind. Own kind. Kind. Kind. Kind."

He continued repeating the final word like an idiot, slowly growing slower and more slurred in his speech. He seemed to gather his last powers for a final appeal. "I'll make it up to you. Please. I didn't mean. I'm coming. I'm . . . " The voice groaned to a stop. A puff of black smoke rose from Apol's chassis. A drone lifted the charred remnants and dropped them in a bucket, then scuttered out of sight carrying them with him.

There was silence in the hall, then Dr. Huer rose and said, "It is over. Justice is done. The traitor is destroyed."

He glanced around the splendid assemblage beneath. "And now, it is my proud honor to proclaim the hero of the hour. Captain Buck Rogers—please step forward."

Although Buck alone had been summoned by Dr. Huer, he took Wilma's hand with one of his, Twiki's with the other. Together they all stepped forward, Dr. Theopolis's lights flashing from his place on Twiki's chest.

"Tell us what reward you wish," Huer said to Buck. "Name it and you shall have it."

"I have it already," Buck replied, turning to clasp Wilma Deering to him.

"Then let the ball begin," Dr. Huer called.

A hidden orchestra struck up the strains of an ancient jazz melody. The elite corps of the Inner City began to receive lessons in ancient boogie dancing from Buck Rogers and Wilma Deering, as the grandest orchestra of the year 2491 belted out the raucous notes of "Chicago, Chicago, that toddlin' town!"